Safe From the Dark

Lily Rede

ISBN: 1479394319
ISBN-13: 978-1479394319

For my writing girls, who never let me stop.

CONTENTS

PROLOGUE

THE SOUNDS OF PASSION were grating – soft murmurs and husky laughter muffled by the partially demolished walls of the house on this side and the sheets of rain pummeling the tarp overhead. It was a good hiding spot, the half-finished addition to the structure – no one would think to look here, and one could listen to every incriminating moment of seduction. *Sin.*

She had come over, despite the rain, and Colin had met her at the door with surprise, exhaustion etched on his face. The poor man needed sleep, but she had talked her way in, her bleached hair artfully tousled, her overblown breasts brushing against him, her breathy voice promising all manner of carnal delights. He was no match for her aggressive overtures – how could he be? He was only a man, and men had needs that had to be fulfilled.

It's not his fault. It's hers, the slut, spreading her legs for any eager cock that came along, luring good men into the muck.

Right now he was probably taking off her tight clothes, filling his hands with her bloated curves, listening to her lies while she gloried in his strength and heat. He had ignored the little warning notes over the last few weeks, letting himself be drawn into sin and decay. He didn't understand. The rage that followed the thought was hot and then icy cold.

Patience. Love is patient. But maybe a stronger warning. Before it's too late.

The red SUV in the driveway glistened in the morning light, its wet lines mocking, like red lips curved in a seductive smile. Like blood.

Above, a sigh of pleasure and a rough male groan.

Wrath.

Mine.

CHAPTER ONE

"SON OF A BITCH!"

Evie Asher swerved to avoid the fallen tree, only to feel the sedan jerk as the tires sank six inches into the mud off the side of what only the most charitable of lunatics would call a road. It was only mid-afternoon, but the thunderclouds and sheets of rain had darkened the October day to twilight and turned the dirt road into sludge. Ten minutes of spinning wheels confirmed her bad luck — stuck fast.

Fucking perfect, Evie thought, and slammed her hand against the steering wheel, instantly regretting it as splinters of pain shot up her aching arm to the partially-healed wounds in her shoulder and side. She had ignored the sling for the trip from New York, finding it awkward to drive one-handed, but after ten hours, even Evie's legendary stamina was giving out and her whole left side was one big, burning ache. She squinted through the rain-slicked windshield at the split road ahead and considered her options. If memory served, her grandmother's cabin was about a mile up the right fork. The nearest neighbors were the Daniels, a half mile down the opposite fork.

Evie had a vague recollection of her Gram taking her to visit Martha Daniels, who smelled of lemon and clean linen, cooing over her and wishing she had a little girl of her own. It was a nice memory, one of Evie's last good ones before her life went to hell. She wondered if Mrs. Daniels would remember her fondly or if disapproval would fill her eyes when she opened the door. If Evie were lucky, she wouldn't remember her at all. Evie had changed,

3

grown up miraculously in one piece, and remade her life as a tough and capable member of the NYPD, until a few weeks ago, when two bullets had knocked her out of commission and her monumentally bad relationship decision had blown up in her face. *Apparently the apple doesn't fall far from the tree.*

The discovery that her grandmother had left her the property in Bright's Ferry, despite everything, had been a welcome surprise. There was a chance the gossip hadn't spread this far. Bright's Ferry was about as rural as you could get, quietly tucked against a secluded New England bay, a good spot to start over. Unless, of course, your parents were at the center of the biggest town scandal in decades. Still, it had been twenty years, and Evie had nowhere else to go.

Maybe this time it will stick, she thought with a sigh.

At the very least, Martha and Hank Daniels would let her use the phone to call the town's lone garage. It was the good human thing to do, regardless of whatever news about her might have made it back to them.

Evie checked her cell phone, unsurprised by the lack of bars, and shoved it into her backpack. There was no way around it, she was going to get soaked. She had never waited around to be rescued, and she wasn't about to start now. Evie took a quick glance around the car, reached for the door handle, and then paused.

You don't need the gun, she reminded her inner cop, who grumbled.

A brief inner struggle and Evie opened the glove compartment, grabbed her 9mm, and awkwardly shrugged into her shoulder holster, gasping in pain. She immediately felt better when the weight of the weapon settled into its customary place, and cautiously eased her hoodie on over it.

One more hour, she promised herself. *One more hour and you'll be lounging in front of a fireplace, drinking a nice pinot*

4

and reading about the dark-eyed Sabatino doing deliciously illicit things to his Contessa on the library floor.

She hefted the backpack onto her good side and stepped out into the rain.

SHIVERING AND COMPLETELY DRENCHED, Evie dropped her backpack on the Daniels' porch. It was a beautiful hundred-year-old farmhouse that was obviously in the process of being restored – scaffolding protected a new wing off the side of the two-story structure. Evie spared only a quick glance around – her teeth were starting to chatter.

Fingers tight with cold, Evie raised a hand to knock.

Nothing.

Come on, come on.

Someone had to be home, judging from the sporty little SUV in the driveway sitting next to a more utilitarian truck. The lights within blazed with beckoning warmth and the smoky scent of a fireplace teased Evie with promises of heat and comfort.

She knocked harder, kicking the door for good measure, stumbling back as it jerked open.

"What the hell, Tom? Can't a guy take one Sunday afternoon – "

He broke off abruptly, hazel eyes widening.

Evie tried to form words, but her brain inconveniently chose that moment to shut down, obviously overloaded by impending hypothermia and the sight of six plus feet of bare, tanned muscle standing in the doorway, clutching a blanket around his waist with lean, elegant hands. His skin had a light sheen of sweat and his dark hair was ruffled over those bright hazel eyes.

Hot.

Even the inner cop whimpered and she gave it a mental shove.

Pull it together, Asher.

"I'm so sorry to bother you, but I was looking for Mr. or Mrs. Daniels – "

His brows snapped together with a frown.

"They're dead. Over a year now. Car accident."

"I'm sorry, I didn't know. I was headed to the old Asher cabin down the road and my car got stuck."

"You were trying to get out there in this?"

Incredulous, he gestured and the blanket slipped just a bit, exposing another inch of taut waist and a narrow pelt of dark hair under his navel that arrowed downward in a most interesting manner.

Evie swallowed and kept her eyes on his.

"I just need a phone to call the garage, if that's okay."

"Colin?" The breathy voice drifting down the stairs had Evie's face heating in a blush, despite her shivers, as her brain stuttered back into working order.

Two cars in the driveway, panting sex god in the doorway. Way to go, Asher. You just cock-blocked your new neighbor.

Said sex god muttered something that sounded suspiciously like, *"Fucking hell,"* and stepped back to let her in.

"Give me five minutes and I'll take you myself."

"You really don't have to do that."

She wavered slightly as she stepped into the warmth of the house, closing her eyes for a moment as heat curled around her frozen limbs. Evie shuddered in reaction.

"Colin!"

The voice was less breathy and more annoyed, and Evie caught a glimpse of a buxom blonde in a blue lace confection on the upstairs landing. It looked uncomfortable, but Evie supposed it wasn't designed to be worn for long. The woman's silicone breasts were clearly trying to make a strategic escape to avoid chafing.

"Wait here while I get some clothes on." He pointed toward a living room, where a fire crackled merrily in the fireplace and the remains of a romantic interlude were strewn on the coffee table – half a bottle of wine, a couple of glasses.

"It's not necessary – "

The sex god paused at the foot of the stairs, impatient.

"Pete Jackson runs the garage by himself, and I'm pretty sure he's got his hands full helping other stranded drivers crazy enough to be out in this mess. I'm not going to make him drop everything to come all the way out here when I can have you over at the Asher cabin in fifteen minutes. Okay?"

Evie started to retort, but then shut her mouth and nodded. She was cranky, wet, and still freezing. If there was ever a time to make her Type-A tendencies take five, this was it. Her half-naked knight in shining blanket turned his back on her and headed up the stairs, treating her to the sight of the strong curve of his spine and more slabs of muscle leading down to what was no doubt a perfectly sculpted ass.

Evie squelched the long-dormant lust circuits that sparked to life and made a bee-line for the fireplace.

"I'M BEING PUNISHED," COLIN muttered as he pulled on jeans in front of a seriously pissed off Deirdre Small. She was busily covering up those bombshell curves she had been so busily baring for him just a little while ago.

Sorry, old buddy, he thought to his poor, neglected cock.

"I knew this wasn't going to happen."

"Come on, Deirdre, this will only take a few minutes. Then I'll be back and we can – "

"I'm not in the mood anymore."

Fully dressed, she glared at him with icy baby blues.

"Last week it was that meeting for the Harvest Festival, and the week before it was the high school pep rally, and the week before that it was that stupid Town Hall meeting that went over by like, six hours. It's always something, Colin!"

"I'm the mayor, Deirdre, remember? You were at the swearing-in?"

"Well, I didn't realize that meant you were never going to fuck me again! You work twenty-four hours a day and now you're skipping sex to go help some stranded tourist?"

"I couldn't just leave her out there. What do you want me to do?"

"Get your priorities straight, Mr. Mayor."

Fluffing her bleached curls, she disappeared into the bathroom and slammed the door.

Colin winced and reached for his boots. Deirdre Small had always been something of a drama queen, but she was eager and available and more interested in his body than in any long-term relationship. Unfortunately, in recent weeks, the sex – when his schedule actually opened up enough to permit such a thing – had become a little boring. Colin couldn't quite pinpoint the problem. She was hot, uninhibited, and always let him take charge. Lately, it just left him a little…uninspired.

He pulled on a sweater and grabbed a clean sweatshirt from a drawer before reaching for his keys and heading back downstairs. Maybe once he took care of his clueless half-drowned guest, Deirdre would be back in the mood to help him burn off some of the stress he'd built up in the six weeks since he'd become mayor of Bright's Ferry. Colin sighed, knowing she'd be out the door by the time his truck cleared the driveway. Irritation sizzled through him and he decided to place the blame squarely on the crazy woman downstairs.

Colin stepped into the living room.

"I thought you might want – "

He stopped short, awareness prickling along every nerve ending. *Talk about inspiration.*

The woman was standing in front of the fireplace, eyes closed, mouth dropped open in pleasure as she absorbed the heat. Her hair was drying to long ribbons of rich brown, and she'd removed the soaked hoodie to reveal a white tank top that lovingly hugged a curvy, compact little body and sweet breasts that would fit his hands to perfection. Colin drank in every line, feeling a little like a voyeur, and then frowned as his eyes landed on the bandages that covered one shoulder and spread down her side.

The frown deepened at the sight of the gun in the holster, lying on the coffee table.

"I hope you have a permit for that."

She looked up as he spoke, her clear gray eyes wide and framed by thick lashes. Her face was devoid of makeup, and she nervously licked a lush lower lip.

"I'm a cop. That is, I was a cop."

God, she's pretty. He hadn't noticed before, but now she was warm and dry, with firelight licking along those sweet curves. The hard punch of lust surprised him, settling low in his abdomen. He struggled to focus on more important things.

"What happened?" He gestured at her bandages.

"It's nothing." She reached for her soaked hoodie, grimacing in distaste.

"Here." Colin stepped forward with the sweatshirt, and for a moment it looked like she was going to turn it down. "Come on, I'm just trying to be helpful."

"I don't need help."

His skepticism must have shown because she had the grace to blush and snatch the sweatshirt from his hands. For a moment, Colin watched her try to pull it over her head, jostling her bad side as little as possible, and trying to smother the little gasps of pain when she moved the wrong way. Rolling his eyes, he stepped forward and carefully untangled her from the fabric. She stiffened immediately. Colin worked on keeping his hands to himself, though his fingers tingled at the accidental brush of soft skin at her waist where her tank rode up. He stepped back.

"Thanks," she muttered grudgingly, "I'm Evie."

The sweatshirt bagged on her, falling to her thighs and slipping off one shoulder as she reached out a hand. Something hot moved through Colin at the sight of her wrapped in his clothes, but he shook it off and enveloped her hand in his, noting the firm grip and graceful fingers.

"Colin Daniels. Welcome to Bright's Ferry."

THE COLD, WET DASH to Colin's truck doused most of the precious warmth Evie had greedily soaked up in front of the fireplace. Her shoulder and side were on fire, and every muscle was tight with exhaustion. She stared out the window of the spacious cab in disbelief at the downpour that showed no signs of letting up.

"Is it always like this?"

"Wait until it starts snowing," Colin grinned, running a hand through his damp hair and cranking the heater, "Mother Nature doesn't do anything by half up here."

Evie noted resentfully that while she probably looked like a wet cat, Colin Daniels still looked like a cover model, with drops of water beading the lashes of those incredible eyes, and more running down his jacket. She was too miserable to really appreciate the fine male specimen in all his hotness, but she wasn't dead yet. Still, she focused her attention out the window as he put the truck in gear and slowly pulled out of the driveway.

"Looks like someone keyed your girlfriend's car pretty badly. Did she report it?"

Colin looked over, frowning at the ugly scratches that marred the cherry red paint on one side of the SUV.

"When did that happen? Shit, she's going to throw a fit."

He shook his head and eased the truck onto the road, carefully making his way back down through the sludge that Evie had plodded through earlier.

"And Deirdre's not – " He cut the statement off abruptly.

She's not what? Not my girlfriend, she's my wife? My mistress? My fuck buddy?

Evie immediately berated herself for being curious one way or another, and readjusted the vents to blast warm air over her chilled skin, burrowing into the borrowed sweatshirt that smelled of clean laundry, cedar, and faintly of a spicy, woodsy aftershave that she told herself didn't care for even as she took another heady breath.

"I'm so sorry to hear about Martha and Hank. What happened?"

"They hit a patch of black ice one night around Christmas and Dad lost control of the car. Did you know them?"

The pain in his voice was not a surprise, but the way he covered it with cool control felt uncomfortably familiar to Evie.

"I met them a couple of times. They were nice." The words were inadequate, but really, what could she say in the face of such blinding loss? "I didn't realize that they had a son."

"I grew up here, but I was in Boston for college and just stayed there. I didn't move back until last year. What about you? Are you – "

"There's my car." Evie wasn't in the mood to answer questions about herself, about her family, or about what had driven her to Bright's Ferry with her tail between her legs. The longer she could avoid talking about it, the better.

Colin didn't pause, but started up the opposite fork.

"Wait, go back! What are you doing?"

"Is there anything in there that you can't go back for when the animals aren't getting ready to board the ark?"

"No, but my suitcase and laptop are in the trunk. An abandoned car is easy pickings."

He pulled his eyes away from the road for a split second to glance at her in disbelief.

"This is Bright's Ferry, not Boston. You could leave the doors wide open with a sign saying, 'Steal Me' and everything would still be there when you got back. Where are you from, anyway?"

"New York," she grudgingly admitted.

"Well, that explains it."

He opened his mouth, no doubt to ask another question, but noted her clenched fingers and the shudders she was trying hard to suppress. He turned up the heater instead.

"We need to get you out of those wet clothes and warmed up."

In another lifetime, Evie would have leapt at the suggestive words and followed it up with a proposal that he see to the job personally. He was tall and broad and hot in a way that was impossible to ignore. However, right now she just wanted a blanket and a serious dose of painkillers. The warm air blasting from the vents slowly permeated the chill in her bones, making her feel lightheaded and unfocused.

"Hang on, we're almost there." His voice was soothing and it almost sounded…worried.

That was much better than the tone of his voice thus far this afternoon. *So bossy. She really didn't need that.* Husky and worried was much better, but Evie couldn't quite wrap her head around it because she was drifting, drifting…

And then the world went black.

CHAPTER TWO

"SHIT." COLIN KEPT ONE hand on the wheel and gently shook his now-unconscious passenger's good shoulder. "Wake up. Hey, can you hear me? Evie?"

Cursing viciously under his breath, Colin stepped on the gas, powering the truck up the last of the muddy incline to the Asher cabin, skidding to a halt in the gravel driveway. He turned to Evie, lightly tapping her cheek. She moaned softly and opened bleary, unfocused eyes.

"Dammit, I should have taken you to a doctor."

"I'm fine," she mumbled, and drifted off again.

Colin unbuckled Evie's seatbelt and tugged her across the bench seat, gathering her up into his arms. She was a soft weight against his chest as he made a mad dash to the porch of the neglected wooden cabin. Dead plants adorned the stairs and a porch swing was dirty and strewn with wet leaves. Settling Evie on the swing's seat, Colin spent a few frustrated minutes searching the planters and the doorframe, finally finding the spare key under a colorful ceramic frog on the railing.

Thank God the lawyer had missed it. At Fran Asher's funeral last April, Colin recalled the sharply-dressed man who had made an appearance with two assistants in tow to box up Fran's things. The attorney had expressed surprise that the whole town had turned out for the funeral of a little old lady who lived alone.

Colin felt a pang of regret as he opened the door and took a breath of stale air. Fran had loved this cabin, and he remembered chopping wood for her as a boy in exchange for lemonade and cookies. Then he'd left for school, ambitious and arrogant and ready to leave the small town behind. By the time he'd returned, Fran was sick, and the town already half in mourning for one of their own. There had been some scandal a few years back, something about Fran's daughter, but Colin had paid little attention, too busy dealing with his own parents' neglected house and getting used to the slower pace of small town life.

He hefted Evie into his arms again, prompting a sound of discomfort, and carried her inside the dark cabin. In the weak afternoon light, Colin maneuvered his way over to a couch covered in a white sheet and set Evie down. She barely noticed. Colin tried a light switch, surprised when the room was flooded with a soft glow. He glanced at the mysterious woman on the couch who had taken the time to ensure that the cabin's electricity was turned on, which meant she was probably planning to stay for a while.

Who is she?

Colin knew he wouldn't get any real answers today, and for the moment there were things to do. The cabin was chilled and unfriendly despite the homey paneled interior. Spacious and comfortable – there was a bedroom on this floor, another upstairs, a small kitchen with a cozy dining area, a wide living room, and a couple of bathrooms. All of the furniture was coated in sheets, with a thick layer of dust.

Colin reached for the cell phone in his back pocket. Not there.

"Shit." It was probably still sitting on the night stand in his bedroom.

He tried the land line, this time not surprised to hear the familiar tone. *Phone service, too.* He dialed.

"Jocelyn? It's Colin. Yes, cats and dogs. It's a mess. Look, I need you to come out to the old Asher cabin right away."

He explained the situation, fielded a few questions, and hung up the phone.

Evie hadn't moved. She looked frail and small, passed out on the couch, and Colin was bemused by the hard knot of worry that was making itself known in his stomach. He busied himself checking the cupboards and found a neglected canister of tea. The kitchen tap ran brown from disuse for a minute, and then cleared. Colin let it run for a few minutes more before filling the kettle he found under the sink. He set the water to heat and turned his attention to the fireplace. A quick check around back revealed that the covered woodpile was fairly dry, and within minutes, Colin had a merry blaze burning. Then he sat down on the couch, his hip nudging Evie's side, and took her hand. Still too cold.

"Evie? Evie, wake up."

He watched as, with effort, she pulled herself to awareness, her gray eyes cloudy with pain. She tried to sit up, and he impulsively put a hand on her stomach to ease her back down, unaware that he was stroking her like a frightened kitten through the sweatshirt.

"Shhh…stay still. I called the doctor. She'll be here in a minute."

"I don't need a doctor."

"We can argue about that later. Right now, I want you to just lie here and get warm while I make some tea, okay?"

The room was warming up, so Colin pulled off his jacket and tucked it around her.

"Stay."

EVIE'S HACKLES ROSE AT the stern command, but she felt like shit, so she'd give him a pass on this one. Besides, the guy had rescued her from drowning and built her a lovely fire that was filling the room and her bones with beautiful, drenching warmth.

His hands felt good.

Thinking about that wasn't productive either, so she focused on getting warm, watching Colin putter around her grandmother's kitchen like he owned the place. She hadn't been here since she was a little girl, and while the bones of the cabin were the same, her grandmother's warm presence was missing, all of her knick knacks and beloved books packed away somewhere.

Probably in the attic, thought Evie, determined to investigate when she felt better. She'd sold most of what she owned, put a few boxes in storage, and the rest of her worldly possessions were in the car, currently stuck in half a foot of mud down the hill. Her knapsack held her holster and gun and a few essentials, and that was it. All of her former life encompassed in a few portable items. Evie swallowed a lump in her throat.

Enough of that, Asher. You're here. You'll put down roots in this town, where Gram lived. Where everyone knew her and loved her, despite what Mom did. Despite what you've done.

A knock had Colin turning off the kettle and opening the door to a small woman in a pink slicker. Her brown hair was damp and curling and shot through with silver, and her face, though a little crinkled, had the sharpest eyes Evie had ever seen. She carried a doctor's kit and a huge bag of takeout, which she unceremoniously shoved at Colin. The mouthwatering aroma of peanut noodles and Tom Yum soup had Evie's stomach growling – it had been hours since lunch.

The woman shrugged off her slicker, handed it to Colin with a pointed glance, and marched over to the couch. Evie carefully pulled herself to a sitting position as the woman perched on the cushion by her hip, taking up her wrist to feel her pulse.

"Well, Evie Asher, I was wondering when you were going to show up."

Evie's jaw dropped.

"How do you know who I am?"

The woman snorted and let go of her wrist to place a cool, firm hand on her forehead.

"Who else would Fran leave the cabin to? Besides, I never forget a baby I brought into this world. Not that one – " she said, jerking her head at Colin, "– and certainly not you. And you're the spitting image of your mother."

Evie's heart sank. Life in Bright's Ferry was going to be difficult if everyone immediately compared her to her mother. Her dismay must have shown on her face, because the woman chuckled.

"Don't look so worried. What's past is past, and you were just a little girl when all that nonsense took place. You're back where you belong."

She tugged Colin's jacket away from Evie's torso.

"I'm Dr. Griggs, but call me Jocelyn. Now, let's see what you've done to yourself."

Evie didn't think to protest as Jocelyn helped her out of the sweatshirt. The doctor frowned at the bandages, noting spots of blood on her side seeping through the white tank top.

"Colin," she said, "See if you can find some sheets and blankets in the boxes in the attic and make up the bed in the guest room. It's closer."

Colin nodded and left the room without a word, though Evie could practically feel his eyes on her, eagerly soaking up every word about her past. *Obnoxious.*

Jocelyn winked.

"Make the man at least buy you dinner before he gets to see your lacy bits."

Evie had no response to that, but let Jocelyn pull her tank top off, peel off her jeans, and then carefully tug back the bandages on her shoulder and side to inspect the damage. She stared for a long moment, but only said, mildly, "Gunshots are nasty things. Shoulder looks okay, but you've popped a few stitches in your side. I hope you're not overly modest. Colin!"

He came downstairs holding a pile of linens and blankets.

"Well, at least the lawyer left all the boxes clearly marked – "

Colin stopped short at the sight of Evie's near nudity and newly healed wounds. Though her underthings were simple and modest, Evie had a sudden desire to cover up as his gaze pierced her from across the room. Instead, she held still as Jocelyn handed her a clean piece of gauze from her bag, instructing her to press it to her side. She gritted her teeth against the sharp stab of pain, but did as she was told while Jocelyn re-dressed her shoulder.

"Is she okay?" Colin set the blankets on the kitchen counter.

"I'm going to need your help. She needs a few stitches. Set up that lamp over here. I need more light."

She glared at Evie, who had the grace to look guilty.

"You have not been taking care of yourself."

Like a chastened teenager, Evie's stubbornness melted in the face of disapproving authority. Normally she would have felt compelled to stand up for herself, but she got the feeling that Jocelyn had this effect on everyone.

"Sorry," she muttered.

Jocelyn moved to the sink to scrub her hands, while Colin repositioned a lamp as ordered.

"Are you always this much trouble, Evie Asher?" he asked softly, his lips quirking in a smile, though his eyes were grim.

Her chin came up.

"Thanks for your help. You can go."

"And have Jocelyn tear off a piece of my hide? I don't think so. Besides, the good mayor doesn't abandon a citizen in need. I'd never hear the end of it."

Evie was shocked.

"You're the mayor? You're too young to be a mayor."

Colin laughed.

"That's what I said when they offered it to me. Dad was mayor for years. After he died, nobody else wanted the job. Then I came home and, well, the Town Council can be pretty persistent..."

"Yes, they pestered him for months. Colin's the prodigal son. Did he tell you?" Jocelyn grinned and pulled on a pair of latex gloves, "He can't walk down the street without some ambitious young woman throwing herself at him."

"Although most of them don't get themselves shot to get my attention." His voice was low and teasing, for Evie's ears only, and she glared at him, ignoring the way his eyes danced.

The last thing you need is to get involved with the mayor. No more high-profile men, Evie Asher, do you hear me? For once, she and the inner cop were in complete agreement.

Her train of thought was interrupted by Jocelyn pulling the bloody gauze away to swab at the wound with something that stung like the devil, and Evie sucked in a pained breath.

"Fucking hell." The words just slipped out.

Jocelyn was matter-of-fact. "I've got some topical anesthetic, but this is still going to hurt like a son of a bitch. I'll work as fast as I can. Colin, sit here."

Colin joined Evie on the couch, letting Jocelyn push and prod them until Colin was supporting her, with Evie grasping his arms while he held her steady, partially tilted on her side.

"Need something to bite down on?"

Evie was ready to reply with a stinging report, until she saw his face – he was serious, and sympathetic. She shook her head.

"Okay, then. Hold on tight."

Jocelyn leaned forward, needle in hand.

STITCHES ARE NOT SEXY, Colin thought to himself as Evie bit her lip and held on, her nails digging into his biceps. Jocelyn's hands were sure as she closed the wound with efficient movements. Even seeing the obscenely torn flesh firsthand, Colin couldn't wrap his head around it. People in his world didn't get shot. But *Evie had been shot.* It was hard to believe anyone would physically harm this beautiful woman, and he reminded himself that she had been NYPD. She was hardly a delicate flower. But when he ignored the jagged wounds that marred her creamy skin, the rest of her didn't exactly scream tough-ass cop. He had to force his eyes to remain on her face, and not drop to her naturally full breasts, not too big or too small, cupped lovingly in simple white lace, or the matching panties, demure and yet disturbingly hot, shaping an ass that he really, *really* wanted a closer look at.

Pretty pervy, Daniels, he thought, *Quit ogling the gunshot victim.*

He wondered what color her nipples were, and his stupid cock twitched behind his zipper, clearly eager to find out whether it made him a total perv or not.

Evie let a whimper past her tightly clenched teeth and Colin suddenly felt like pond scum.

"Almost there," he murmured.

Ten minutes later they were done, and Jocelyn smoothed a new sterile bandage over the stitches. Evie was shaking, damp with sweat, and clearly exhausted, and accepted the painkillers Jocelyn handed her, gulping them down with half a mug of tepid tea. Colin was equally shaken, but hurried to make up the bed in the spare room and get the electric heater going, and then returned in time to hear the last of Jocelyn's lecture.

"…and when I say take it easy, I mean it, or you're going to wind up with a lot worse than a mild fever and a few popped stitches. Colin, can you help Evie get to bed?"

Colin didn't give Evie a chance to argue, but scooped her up into his arms, careful of her wounds, trying to ignore her long legs and softer than soft skin against his hands. She held herself stiffly until he set her gently on the bed and pulled sheets and a handmade blazing star quilt up over her, gently tucking her in. Her eyes clouded with confusion as he impulsively stroked a lock of hair back from her face, savoring the silken strand against his fingers, which he was sure his prickly new neighbor would never let him get away with if she weren't drugged and off her game.

"Get some sleep."

Her eyes were already drifting shut as he reached for the lamp switch and then softly shut the door behind him.

Jocelyn was packing up her equipment, shaking her head.

"Frannie would be spinning in her grave if she knew that little girl had gotten herself shot up like that. I assume you're staying?"

"I – uh – "

"Take the couch. Those painkillers will knock her out for a good long stretch. Make sure she eats when she gets up, but don't let her overdo it for the next couple of days."

"Jocelyn, I've got a million things to do tomorrow. I can't – "

The diminutive doctor paused in the middle of pulling on her slicker to poke him in the chest. Hard.

"You will stay and help this young woman, Colin Daniels. This community is going to welcome her with

open arms or so help me God, you're all going to answer
to me."

Colin was shocked by her vehemence. Jocelyn
could be stern, but she almost never lost her cool.

"What happened to her?"

"The gunshots? I have no idea, and she doesn't
seem to be the type to share. What I do know is that after
what happened with her mother, she deserves all the
goodwill we can muster."

She rolled her eyes impatiently at Colin's blank
look.

"You were away from Bright's Ferry too long. Do
you remember Fran's daughter, Laura?"

"Not really."

"You were barely a teenager when it all happened.
Years ago, after Frannie's husband passed away, Laura
married Phil McCann and moved to Boston. She never
liked it here, and they only brought Evie back to visit Fran
once a year or so, under duress. Phil was an alcoholic and
from what Fran said, Laura was miserable from day one,
but too proud to admit she'd made a mistake. So she
started popping pills to cope, and it just got worse from
there – paranoia, rages. I remember seeing Evie when she
was about five – underfed, scared of her own shadow.
What a travesty."

"So then what happened?"

"When Evie was seven, Laura brought her to stay
with Fran, and said that she wanted to get into rehab. Phil
was cheating on her, and she wanted to make a new life for
the two of them. Frannie was so relieved."

Jocelyn wiped away a tear, and Colin started
forward, but stopped as Jocelyn held up a hand.

"Laura left Evie with Fran to go take care of some
things and the rest – well, it was all in the papers. She
caught Phil and his mistress in that crappy motel across
the bay and put a couple of bullets in them before turning
the gun on herself. Phil survived, that bastard, and came

back for Evie. And Frannie never saw her again. She sent money and letters, but who knows if Evie ever got them, or what kind of a life she had after that. Fran even consulted a lawyer, but there was nothing she could do. She never really forgave herself."

Colin ignored her sputtering and wrapped the doctor in a hug. She caved and patted him on the back.

"Your charms don't work on me, Colin Daniels," she said, watery, "Save it for the pretty young things."

She pulled back, but narrowed her eyes at him.

"Be nice to Evie Asher, but keep your hands to yourself, got it? She doesn't need to be added to your list of playthings. That girl deserves more than a quick fuck in the front of your pickup."

Colin could feel the heat rising in his cheeks, but nodded. No matter how delicious and lickable Evie looked in or out of her clothes, she clearly was not easygoing or casual, eager and/or grateful for a roll in the sheets. She came with epic amounts of baggage, and it only took one afternoon for him to see that he would be smart to keep far, far away. Evie Asher was trouble.

CHAPTER THREE

THE EARLY MORNING SUNLIGHT
streaming through the window was a surprise, and Evie
squinted at the unfamiliar surroundings for a moment
before memory came flooding back – the storm, the
doctor, and the too-attractive-for-his-own-good mayor
who had lifted her like she weighed nothing and tucked
her into bed with strong, warm hands.

None of that, she reminded herself.

Evie pushed back the quilt and carefully sat up,
taking stock of her injuries. Her shoulder was stiff, but not
terrible, and her side throbbed, but the pain wasn't
unmanageable. She found that someone had thoughtfully
set a bottle of ibuprofen next to the bed with a glass of
water, and gratefully gulped two as she looked around the
room – heartlessly bare save for the night stand and the
bed, the guest room was still pretty, with blue patterned
wallpaper dappled with lovely morning light. Through the
windows, a magnificent view of the bay stretched out far
below. Evie pulled herself to her feet, clutching the iron
bedpost until her balance reasserted herself.

Her suitcase and laptop sat by the door, along
with a pile of towels – another pleasant surprise. Evie felt a
twinge of guilt. She hadn't been at her best yesterday, and

while she was perfectly capable of taking care of herself, she had to admit that her night would have been worse without Colin's take-charge attitude. If she was planning to live here, she had to make friends. She shouldn't let herself become irked by the mayor's high-handedness or his annoyingly sexy smile.

I'll call and thank him. Later. Shower first.

The thought of hot water pushed Evie to gather clean clothes and towels and make her way into the connecting bathroom. Ten minutes later she was standing half under the hot spray, blissfully rinsing shampoo from her hair while she carefully kept her bandages dry. The water did wonders for her stiff muscles, and while Evie pulled on jeans and a soft cream-colored sweater, she was amazed at how much better she felt after a good night's sleep. Squeezing the excess water from her hair, she ran a quick brush through it, her mind on breakfast.

She stepped into the living room and stopped short.

Colin Daniels was sitting at her kitchen table, drinking tea and reading the newspaper like he belonged there. He was still in the same clothes from yesterday, but he'd obviously showered, his dark hair still damp. Evie tried to ignore the idea of Colin in the upstairs shower, soapy and hot, but a quick, shocking pulse of interest had her clenching her thighs.

"Hey, you're up!" He smiled and set the paper down.

"I thought you'd be gone by now." Okay, that wasn't the best thing to blurt out when trying to make a fresh start. Clearly Colin didn't think so either, as one eyebrow went up and the smile vanished. Evie took a fortifying breath and tried again.

"Sorry, I'm not quite awake yet. Thank you for getting my things. And for calling the doctor. I didn't realize that I'd pushed myself so hard. I was in a hurry to get up here."

Colin considered her for a long moment, and then smoothly got to his feet, the easy smile returning to his face.

"Anytime. I polished off the Thai, so there's nothing left to eat unless you like baking soda or rat poison. I can run into town and pick up a few things."

"Don't worry, I'll be fine. I just need to get my car – "

But Colin was shaking his head.

"You're going to need a tow truck to pull it out, and Pete's not going to be able to make it up until this afternoon."

Evie blew out a frustrated breath, and Colin grinned.

"You've been in the city too long. Things up here take time."

"It's going to take a while to get used to that," Evie admitted.

"Jocelyn said to take it easy, so why don't you just hang out – "

"Look, I can't just sit around all day – it's not me. But you don't need to babysit. I've got a bunch of errands to run. If you wouldn't mind dropping me in town, I can find my own way back."

Colin shook his head, laughing.

"How about a compromise? Let's go to Mary's and get some breakfast, and then you can run your errands and stock up. When you're ready to go, I'll give you a ride and make sure you don't collapse on the way back up the hill. It's close to home anyway. Deal?"

Evie only hesitated a moment before shaking his hand, and wondered if he felt the tingle where their skin touched.

"Sure. Thanks."

She started to pull her hand back, but he held on, tugging her a little closer.

"Evie," he said softly, "I don't know what happened to you, but it's a small community. We look out for each other. I hope that someday you'll feel at home here."

He let her go and started for the door, leaving her to follow, sudden tears pricking behind her eyes.

I'm a mess, she thought as she grabbed a jacket and hurried after him. She was so used to judgment and condemnation that she had no idea how to react to simple kindness anymore. Everyone had an agenda. Everyone wanted something from her, ready to pounce on the slightest hint of vulnerability or weakness. So she didn't show any. She didn't rely on anyone if she could help it, but Colin's gentle voice and warm hands made her wonder if she could move past her hang-ups, maybe start learning to trust people again. The thought was too scary, so she pushed it aside and followed Colin out to the car.

The road down to town was muddy, but a million times better than the day before, and Evie drank in the sight of the little town below. Bright's Ferry was squashed between its own little bay and a generous hill that the townies affectionately called their "mountain." Many of the newer residents lived in town, but the families that had been here for generations had settled in the hills, the winding roads still mostly unpaved. A hundred years ago, this had been a fishing town, and a few trawlers and small fisheries remained, though, like much of the area, the town relied on B&Bs and passing tourists in search of cute little weekend getaways.

Evie ignored Colin's surreptitious glances at her from behind the wheel and permitted herself a tiny moment of self-congratulation. *She'd done it.* She'd left her old life behind – the scandal and pain, the humiliation and lack of professionalism. And the betrayal. That was the worst. The shimmering bay and the town faded from view as she thought back to New York and the night that changed everything.

She'd been three weeks away from the detective's exam. After years of struggle, holding down two jobs to survive long enough to get through school and the academy, never relying on anyone for anything, her goal was in sight. She'd stubbornly cared for her father as his alcoholism progressed – the angry, abusive man who once ground her self-esteem into the dirt now reduced to a feeble addict in hospice care – and finally buried him without a tear. Evie couldn't celebrate, though Jack had urged her to, insisting that the burden of her childhood was behind her now that the bastard was dead.

Intelligent and self-assured, protective and flattering, handsome Captain Jack Forrest seemed to offer everything that her shattered family never gave her, and for two months she'd had a heady, secret affair with the soon-to-be-divorced police captain. It was hot. It was intense. It was so incredibly against the rules. Evie didn't care, reveling in the kind of connection she had denied herself for so long.

The night she buried her father, Evie felt numb and off-center. Annoyed, Jack reminded her that had snuck away from the Governor's charity ball to find her before her shift for a quick fuck in her tiny apartment. Evie remembered that last time – he hadn't bothered to take off his tux, and the light gleamed off his wedding ring as he thrust into her, not bothering to make sure came, like he usually did. When they were done, unsatisfied and uncertain, Evie made the mistake of wondering out loud how the divorce was proceeding – he and his wife did a good job of keeping up appearances in public. For the sake of his career, of course.

I've got it under control, Evie. Quit hounding me.

Jack won the argument – he always did – reminding her that if she loved him, she'd be patient, and she headed off to work, hoping to put the latest tiff behind them. She loved him. He loved her, despite her family history. Everything would be fine.

It was in the precinct bullpen, as Evie checked her gear, that her world imploded. In a blue satin gown, Brianne Forrest stormed in, diamonds gleaming at her wrists and throat, and demanded to know why Evie, a lowly patrol cop, was fucking her husband, who was out of her league in more ways than one. Evie, shocked, turned to Jack, in tow like a chastened puppy. Trying to ignore the disapproval of her fellow officers, she waited for Jack to defend her, to step up and tell the truth.

He looked away.

And she knew. Blinded by her emotions and longing for the care she'd missed since she was a girl, she'd let herself be used, let herself believe that he really wanted her, wanted a life with her. She'd believed that the marriage was over, that he was a sad man keeping up appearances, and fallen for the whole thing, hook, line, and sinker. The sudden clarity left her breathless, but she managed to pull herself together and make it out to her black and white, the silent condemnation from her partner, Simone Behr, worse than the official punishment that was sure to come – fraternizing with a superior officer was strictly prohibited.

Heartbroken and shaky, Evie was distracted, and it nearly cost her her life as they chased two scumbag drug dealers through Central Park later that night. She tackled one to the ground, securing his piece, but missed the backup in his ankle holster, and he struggled, freeing one hand, and then –

Bang! Bang!

Evie woke in the hospital, in agony. The wounds would heal, but her reputation would not. With his connections, Jack would get a slap on the wrist, but Evie's career with the NYPD was over. She was suspended, pending an investigation into the allegations. Her coworkers stopped speaking to her, Simone wouldn't answer the phone. Lying in the hospital bed, she thought back to the last time she'd been truly happy, and remembered Gram – her soft hands, the peace and quiet of the cabin, and the wide ocean stretched out below.

After Gram's death, there had been a call from her lawyer that she had never bothered to return. Her father had severed all contact, and as an adult, Evie worried that too much time had passed to reconnect, and then lost her chance when word of Gram's death reached her. She called the lawyer back. Hope and purpose washed over her the moment she hung up the phone.

Even gone, Gram was giving her another chance at a home.
"Everything okay?"

Evie snapped back to the present and the handsome young mayor pulling into a space in front of the town's modest Town Hall. For a moment, she wondered what kind of a man he was when he wasn't rescuing half-drowned damsels who showed up on his doorstep, but then forcefully reminded herself that it didn't matter. She wanted to be friendly, but her reaction to Colin so far had her worried. Very worried. He could be a prince, a playboy, or a Boy Scout. She wasn't going to give herself a chance to get close enough to find out.

"Fine. I'm dying for a cup of coffee."

"Why don't I meet you in the diner in half an hour? Right over there. I'm going to check in at the office and make sure nothing exploded in the eighteen hours I've been gone."

He rolled his eyes, and flashed a grin as he left her on the sidewalk. Evie steeled herself, letting the peal of church bells in the distance wash over her, and then crossed the square toward the old-fashioned Sheriff's Department on the corner.

COLIN BREEZED INTO HIS office, not surprised to find Candace Wilkinson there ahead of him. In her mid-forties, Candace had run the mayor's office for twenty-five years, and no one knew the ins and outs of Bright's Ferry like she did. His assistant, Tom Castillo, often complained that between Colin's need to handle everything himself and Candace's efficiency, he had nothing left to do, but Candace was indispensable. With impeccable but severe style, Candace was a formidable presence in Town Hall, and Colin was often grateful for her ability to run interference for him.

"Isn't it Sunday, and weren't you and Alan going antiquing this weekend?"

Candace merely handed over a stack of messages, unruffled.

"Alan sprained his wrist fixing the door to the barn, so we had to postpone. Besides, I knew you'd be in sooner or later. One call from the Harvest Festival Committee, one complaint from the Harbormaster about college kids drinking on the docks – he wants that ordinance to go through so he can put up signs."

"Yeah, I know. It's got to go to the Council first."

"One call from Millicent Grayson."

Candace glared at him and Colin felt his cheeks heating. Millicent was sweet, a young mother who had lost her husband in a fishing accident on one of the local trawlers. He'd helped her through her loss, comforted her young son, but so far had managed to resist her not so subtle hints that he could comfort her best in bed. He had a feeling that the guilt involved would far eclipse the pleasure of fucking the pretty young woman – nothing easy or uncomplicated there.

"I'm not leading her on, Candace, I swear."

Candace humphed, but continued.

"Tom went over to talk to Dreyer Morton."

"What's wrong now?"

"Apparently the neighbors' trees are dropping apples on his precious roses."

"Does he realize that's not really an issue for this office?"

"He's the richest man in town, and this is Bright's Ferry. Everything's an issue for this office. Two calls from

31

Deirdre Small. She says you're not answering your cell phone."

Colin sank into his desk chair.

"I know. I left it at home last night. Is that it?"

Candace raised an eyebrow, but didn't comment. Instead, she pulled an envelope from a drawer, addressed to him in crude charcoal strokes.

"Another one of these."

"What does it say this time?"

"The usual about the wages of sin and corruption. What do you want to do with it?"

"Put it in the box with the others. Just some nutjob trying to cause trouble."

Candace frowned.

"This is the third this month, and if you don't mind my saying so, it sounds a little more...emphatic...than the others."

"I don't want to feed this guy's ego by catering to his delusions, Candace. Just ignore it. He'll stop eventually. What else?"

Candace plopped a stack of paper on his desk.

"Just a few signatures and you're out of here. Everything okay? You seem distracted," she noted, curious.

Colin thought of Evie's bright gray eyes and prickly demeanor, and a flare of arousal flickered up his spine. But he only waved, dismissive.

"I'm fine. Let's do this."

Picking up a pen, he dove in.

EVIE SIZED UP THE man sitting across from her. Dressed in jeans and an oxford with a badge clipped to his belt, Sheriff Tony Arnetto was tall, broad, with dark Italian looks that probably had more than one woman lingering on the old cliché about a man in uniform. However, the fantasy usually didn't include a pair of chocolate brown eyes that seemed to brim with perpetual grief. A man that handsome shouldn't look so sad.

"Evelyn Asher."

"It's Evie." *God, I'm nervous.*

Tony drummed his fingers on the desk and considered her thoughtfully.

"They don't have very nice things to say about you back in New York. Jack Forrest and I came up in the academy together. Word gets around."

Evie braced herself for the rejection. It had been lunacy to think she could start over as a small town deputy, but law enforcement was what she knew, what she was good at. Evie's eyes fell to the desk, absently noting a wedding picture of Tony with a gorgeous redhead.

It might be time to hone your waitressing skills, Asher.

"The man was a prick." Tony's voice was sharp.

Startled, Evie's eyes snapped up to meet Tony's, which were full of sympathy.

"Once a prick, always a prick. Still, I gotta say, the last few weeks don't show the greatest judgment on your part."

"I know. I've basically been in free fall." There wasn't anything to do but admit it.

"How's the shoulder?"

"Good," she lied, "Barely notice it anymore."

Tony smiled wryly.

"You're a bad liar."

He leaned back, crossing his arms.

"Here's the deal. This is a tiny department, just me and the rookie – Zeke Biggs. We get our fair share of shit, mostly during tourist season and the Harvest Festival, which is coming up, so the extra hands would be helpful. I have a feeling you burned a lot of bridges – "

Evie swallowed a lump in her throat and pointed at the computer screen, where her entire history was laid out in black and white.

"Look at my records from before. I had the highest collar rate in the precinct, not a black mark or a single infraction. I was three weeks from taking the detective exam – "

"And then you blew it all for a little fun in the sack with God's gift to douchebaggery."

Evie stuttered to a halt, and then –

"Not my finest hour. We all make mistakes."

Tony rubbed his gold wedding ring absently.

"Yes, we do."

Evie lifted her chin, determined.

"But I think it's safe to say that all that shit is over with and I've certainly learned my lesson."

Tony's laugh surprised her. He stood.

"Your Gram was the nicest woman I ever met, and it broke her heart, what happened to your mom. She always knew you'd come back here one day. I don't want to be the one to meet her in the afterlife as the guy who wouldn't give her little Evie a job."

A kernel of hope blossomed in Evie's chest.

"So – "

"Why don't we call this a trial? The pay's crap, the hours are irregular, and Zeke is still wet behind the ears."

"Sounds great."

Tony held out a hand.

"Welcome aboard, Evie Asher."

CHAPTER FOUR

If it weren't for her wounded side, Evie would have skipped down the stairs of the building, her shiny new badge clipped to her belt, the familiar weight of a holster against her hip. Tony had given her strict orders to recuperate for at least a week.

Thanks, Gram, Evie thought to herself, grateful for the goodwill her grandmother had managed to accrue over the years. She only hoped she could live up to her legacy.

Evie couldn't help the grin that played around her lips as she stepped up to the homey diner across the street. It had been too long since she'd had anything to smile about.

"Tiny, come *down!*" The voice was plaintive and a little panicked.

Evie paused and looked around, spotting the source of the complaint – a little blond boy, about nine years old, staring up into the branches of a giant tree halfway down the block. She judged the height of the tree as the child flung himself against the trunk, managed to get a foothold, and started up. Six laboring feet up, he slipped, skidded, and landed at the base with a thud.

"Ow."

As he dusted himself off to try again, Evie joined him.

"What's the matter?"

"Tiny's stuck,"

Big blue eyes, brimming with tears, met hers as he pointed. Evie looked up to see what had to be the fattest striped furball in the state clinging to a branch about twenty feet up, yowling his head off.

"Hmmm."

Evie reached into her pocket, dug out a dollar, and pointed at the market.

"Why don't you go over there and pick up a can of tuna, and we'll see if we can't get him down, okay?"

"Mama says I'm not supposed to talk to strangers."

"That's good advice. I'm Evie. I'm a Sheriff's deputy."

She showed him her badge, which he inspected carefully, eyes wide.

"Can I help you, Miss?" The girlish voice didn't match the petite woman striding over to join them. Dressed in Gothy black lace and heavy military boots, her purple streaked reddish hair and heavy rocker makeup were at odds with the little glasses perched on the end of a decidedly cute nose.

"Brian Olsen, where's your mom?"

"Getting her nails done. Tiny got stuck."

"Again?" The unusual young woman sighed.

"Where's a hot firefighter when you need one, right?" Evie joked, and nodded at little Brian, who scampered off toward the market. She held out her hand.

"Hi, I'm Evie Asher."

The woman stared.

"Good Lord, you're Fran's granddaughter."

She shook hands, her grip firm.

"Welcome to Bright's Ferry. I'm Grace Mallow. I run the library."

"Really?" The disbelief slipped out, and Evie instantly regretted it as a shadow passed over Grace's face. "Sorry, I didn't mean that – you're just so – young."

Grace took it in stride, but Evie was relieved as Brian came scampering back with a can of tuna and a can opener.

"Great, let's give this a try."

She opened the tuna, and within seconds, the fat monster had wiggled his way down the tree trunk and was devouring bites of fish in between rapturous squeezes from the little boy.

"Nice job, Ms. Asher." Grace grinned.

"She's a deputy!" filled in Brian, helpfully.

"I just moved to town."

"And you're already rescuing cats from trees. Well, the least I can do is buy breakfast for one of Bright's Ferry's finest."

"There are only three of us."

"All the more reason to keep your strength up."

She led the way into the diner, which was overflowing with locals and tourists – families, groups of little old women, and a table full of fishermen, trading stories and downing massive plates of eggs and home fries.

Evie noted the cold looks darted their way and for a moment wondered if this is what it would always be like – suspicion and judgment from complete strangers – until she realized that the looks of disapproval were aimed at *Grace*. To her credit, Grace ignored them and claimed a booth in the corner. In seconds, a tiny woman in a uniform and apron approached the table. Wrinkled and ancient, her eyes still sparkled. She reminded Evie of an aging fairy, minus the wings.

"Why Evie Asher, as I live and breathe. You're the spitting image of your mother, God rest her soul."

Evie was shocked as the tiny woman enveloped her in a hug, her limbs surprisingly strong for her pixie-like size.

"Evie, this is Mary. She owns this place."

"You used to sit up at that counter and suck down a cherry shake faster than any kid I ever met." Mary let Evie go and patted her on the shoulder. Evie suppressed the wince as she jarred her wound.

"I don't remember that."

"You were just a little thing. Frannie would be so happy that you've come back to town."

"Tony gave Evie a job." Grace grinned.

"Tony gave Evie a what?" The male voice was stern and frankly disbelieving.

Evie looked up to see Colin striding toward them, looking pissed. He ignored the welcomes and well-wishes from the locals.

Popular. Evie filed that away and braced herself for an argument.

"A job. As a deputy."

"Why would he do a fool thing like that? Move over, Gracie, honey."

Grace obligingly scooted down to make room for him, allowing Colin to sit across from Evie, the better to glare at her disapprovingly, she supposed. He and Grace were clearly friends, but Evie didn't detect any romantic interest.

"Because I haven't won the lottery lately and everybody needs to work?" Evie was defensive, but the irritation in those hazel eyes made her want to shrink into her seat. It didn't help that the diner's occupants were watching them with open fascination.

"You need to recover."

"It's none of your business." Evie was furious, but kept her voice low.

Mary cuffed Colin on the back of the head.

"Ow. What was that for?" Colin rubbed his head.

"Let the girl have a cup of coffee before you start reorganizing her life. And Dreyer was in here earlier.

Something about his neighbors and your lack of control as mayor being a symptom of your deficiencies as a man."

Evie choked on a laugh, but covered it with a cough as Colin glared at her.

"I know all about it, Mary, but thanks for being the town crier."

"Pancakes all around," said Grace, "And don't skimp on the bacon!"

"Sure thing, sweetie." Mary vanished with a last wink at Evie.

Evie knew she should leave it alone, but she couldn't resist.

"Sheriff Arnetto wouldn't have agreed to take me on if he didn't think I was up for the job."

"Tony's stretched thin. He'd hire a rodeo clown if one came knocking."

"I'm a damned good cop." Evie struggled to keep her voice down, but it wasn't easy.

"If you're such a good cop, why aren't you still making the streets of New York safe for the citizens there instead of up here with two bullet holes in your body?"

"You got shot? You're from New York?" Evie couldn't tell which question Grace found more exciting, but she was practically squirming in her seat. "I love New York. Love it, love it, love it. Why would you ever leave?"

Thankfully, three plates piled high with steaming pancakes and bacon arrived, along with a heavenly mug of coffee, and Evie avoided answering either question by stuffing her face. Colin attacked his pancakes, irritation oozing off of him, while Grace launched into an account of her only trip to the city to see one of her favorite Goth bands play a nightclub. Evie nodded and smiled at the right places, amused by the young woman's enthusiasm, but she couldn't concentrate, her mind on Colin's annoyance, her senses focused on where his knee brushed her thigh beneath the table.

Move your leg, Asher.

She'd barely been in town a day, and already she was a little fascinated by a good-looking, take-charge kind of guy who knew just how to push her buttons. Evie sucked it up. So she had a type, so what? It meant nothing. Right now, the focus was healing, starting her new path, and keeping men like Colin Daniels from ruining her life. Again.

Grace's running commentary was interrupted by a severe-looking woman entering the diner, scanning the tables until she spotted them.

"Hi Candace." Grace sat up a little straighter, unconsciously smoothing her hair as Candace gave her a dismissive once-over.

"Colin, Deirdre Small would like a word. She cornered me in the office just as I was leaving."

Colin stopped glaring at Evie long enough to look up, puzzled.

"Tell her I'm in here."

"She wants a word. Outside. In private." Candace's pinched mouth was clear indication of what she thought about that. She glanced at her watch. "Alan needs his medicine. I'll see you tomorrow..."

With barely a glance at Evie or Grace, she turned on her heel and marched out.

"Fuck," Colin muttered under his breath, and then pulled out a handful of cash and dropped it on the table. "Breakfast is on me. I'll meet you by the truck in a few, Evie."

Ten minutes later, Evie emerged from the diner full of pancakes, with Grace's phone number in her pocket and the promise of a girls' night in the near future. She had never been good at making friends, but the quirky librarian seemed like a kindred spirit – a possible real connection. Evie's good mood lasted until she started toward the market, past the alley next to the diner, where Deirdre had what looked like a very willing Colin pressed up against the brick, her tongue down his throat, her curves pressed against him.

Evie stopped short. For a split second, she imagined herself in Deirdre's place, her body pressed against all that muscled heat, Colin's hands coursing over her, tilting her head for the fit of his mouth, tugging a fistful of her hair back so he could taste her throat, rocking his hips against hers.

Hot and unnerved, Evie shook her head and hurried away.

COLIN SAW EVIE PUSHING a loaded cart toward his truck and hurried to help her.

"I would have fetched you."

"I got it."

He brushed aside her attempts to help and quickly loaded the bags into the pickup.

"Looks like you're stocked up for the winter. What's next, burying nuts in the backyard?"

"Funny. You should go on the road."

Walking by, clutching the fat feline he called Tiny, little Brian Olsen spotted them and waved furiously.

"Bye, Deputy Evie!"

Evie waved back, smiling.

"Making friends already?" Colin chuckled.

She turned her grin on him and he realized it was the first time she'd really smiled at him, a genuine smile. He liked it. More than he should.

They both reached for the cart at the same time and collided, and for a second, they were pressed together, eyes locked. Colin felt sucker-punched by her softness and the heat that filled his groin, but jerked away before she could notice him harden against her.

Shit. First Deirdre, and now this. Stop letting your dick lead the way, Daniels.

Colin quickly returned the cart and then joined Evie in the truck. The air was heavy and awkward, and he turned on the radio, letting music fill the void as he reflected that his life had gotten messy this weekend.

Deirdre had apparently decided that Colin's abandonment yesterday was the last straw. For the first time in their dalliance, she was sinking her claws in, apparently ready for more than just a quick release of sexual tension once in a while. Colin was pretty sure that was a bad idea. For all their physical compatibility, he and Deirdre didn't spend much time talking – they simply didn't have anything in common outside of a mutual appreciation for her curves. Pointing that out only made Deirdre eager to prove him wrong, and somehow Colin found that he had a date – an honest-to-God *date* – for tomorrow night. With Deirdre.

Suddenly he felt very tired.

If he felt it, Evie looked it. Her mouth was tight, the dark circles under her eyes making them look huge against her face.

"You overdid it this morning."

"I'm okay," she insisted, stifling a yawn, "Thank you for taking me into town."

She looked small and alone when he left her at the cabin a few minutes later, having helped her carry everything inside and assuring her that Pete would drop off her car later. He couldn't help wondering about her as he made the short drive to his own place.

She doesn't have a boyfriend. Of that, he was fairly certain. Besides the fact that she wouldn't be up here, all by herself and injured to boot, a guy would need a freaking tall ladder to scale the spiked walls she'd built around herself. Colin tamped down on the sneaking suspicion that behind those walls was something soft and hot and delicious, and the growing temptation to find the crack in her shields that would let him delve inside for a taste.

THE BLONDE SLUT HAD him in her clutches again, this time out in the open, uncaring who saw her run her filthy hands over him. They'd argued in the alley, and it was pleasing to hear Deirdre rail about the scratches on her precious car. Less pleasing was Colin's soothing tone. Deirdre had pouted, touching his chest and batting her fake eyelashes at him, and he'd barely protested when she'd pinned him against the wall to take what she wanted.

Yesterday's warning was obviously not enough.

Something would have to be done.

EVIE SLEPT FOR MOST of the day, rousing herself to make lunch and pull the sheets off the furniture. Most of it was still in the attic, and Evie wondered if she could hire some of the local teens to help her haul it downstairs. She'd moved her things up into Gram's old room. With a little TLC and some new wallpaper, it would soon feel like home.

In the late afternoon, Evie tugged on her favorite hoodie over a tank top, wrapped herself in a blanket, and settled on the porch swing to nurse a cup of cider while she watched the sun go down in a blaze of bright oranges and purples. She felt peaceful and content for the first time in ages, only a little troubled by the thought of Colin's gorgeous hazel eyes. She was still thinking about them as she dozed off, cocooned in her blanket against the autumn chill.

When Evie woke, the sky across the hill was orange. Disoriented, she sat up.

That's not right.

Night had clearly fallen, and the lights of the town winked in the darkness. In the other direction she could see the faint glow of Colin's house.

But across the hill, the sky was *orange.*

Then she smelled it.

"Oh my God."

Fire.

Evie scrambled out of her blanket, nearly crashing face first as her feet got tangled in the folds. She raced inside for keys and phone and the new fire extinguisher she'd bought only that morning, and then dove into her car.

"Call nine-one-one," she ordered the voice activation on her phone. It beeped, searching for a signal.

"Shit!"

Evie careened across the hill, taking backroads, forced to double back a few times until she finally spotted it – a pretty little house in a clearing, one side engulfed in flames. A couple of nearby trees were on fire, but thankfully, the house was situated against the rocky part of the hill. That didn't mean that the fire couldn't or wouldn't jump, but it might buy the fire department some time to get up here.

Evie screeched to a halt and jumped out of the car. Her extinguisher wasn't going to be much help. Relief coursed through her as she heard sirens in the distance – finally, someone had noticed.

Tomorrow I'm switching cell phone plans.

A cry from the house had Evie swearing viciously under her breath, and her eyes widened as she noticed the scratched red SUV in the driveway.

Deirdre.

Not giving herself time to change her mind, Evie soaked her hoodie in a brimming planter by the porch, silently thanking the skies for last night's deluge. She gasped as the wet fabric hit her skin. Covering her nose and mouth, Evie kicked open the door, which had just started to catch. Her eyes stung at the blast of heat and smoke. Trying hard not to breathe, she forced her way inside.

"Deirdre? Ms. Small? I'm with the Sheriff's Department. I'm going to get you out!"

"Help!"

Evie raced up the stairs, which creaked ominously, the bannister on fire.

She found Deirdre trapped in her bedroom. A few blasts from the fire extinguisher doused enough flames for Evie to get the door open. In a skimpy robe and a pair of slippers, Deirdre was crouched in the corner of the girly room desperately trying to keep the flames away as she swatted ineffectually at them with a towel. She squealed as Evie crashed her way inside.

"Come on!"

Evie yanked off her wet hoodie and wrapped it around Deirdre, practically dragging her toward the stairs. Deirdre took one look at the flaming bannister, the staircase now smoldering, and panicked.

"I can't!"

"You have to!"

Deirdre struggled as Evie tried to force her down the stairs. Dammit, the woman was stronger than she looked. Evie finally shook her, hard.

"Do you want to die in here?!?"

Terrified, Deirdre shook her head.

Evie coughed and started down first, keeping a tight grip on Deirdre's arm.

"Just follow me and we'll be okay."

Suddenly, the house *groaned*, and the heat seemed to increase as something *crashed* above them, letting loose a shower of sparks.

Deirdre screamed.

"Move!"

Evie propelled Deirdre down the stairs as the house started to collapse, the heat and smoke intense. She couldn't see the door. Something heavy and hot glanced off her wounded shoulder, setting off a blinding wave of agony. Deirdre clutched Evie, terrified, and Evie started to panic herself, because *she still couldn't see the door.*

Suddenly, Evie ran headfirst into a wall. It had to be a wall, but then the wall *moved,* and strong arms gripped the two women, pulling them toward the light and air outside. Barely clear of the house, Deirdre dropped into a dramatic faint, leaving the firefighter to catch her. Gulping air, Evie stumbled forward a few steps, dropped to her hands and knees, and promptly threw up.

COLIN SLAMMED THE DOOR of his truck and grimly made his way toward the collection of ambulances and fire trucks in the clearing in front of Deirdre's house. The fire was well contained, but a team of firefighters still worked to put it out completely. The air was acrid with smoke and burned wood. The call from Tom had prepared him, but he still felt uneasy and upset enough to tear someone's head off, his composure shredded by the spike of adrenaline and fear.

He spotted Deirdre immediately and relaxed a fraction. Wrapped in a blanket, sitting on a gurney, she was busy making a huge fuss as an EMT bandaged a bloody gash on her shapely thigh. Colin scanned the area and was unprepared for the wave of relief that swamped him when he saw Evie, one hip propped against the back bumper of an ambulance as she held an oxygen mask over her face and nodded at whatever firefighter Matt Harris was saying. His stomach tight, Colin hurried over.

"Evie."

"Hey, Colin." Matt held out a hand, engulfing his own in a firm shake. The guy was a former All State linebacker, and a blond giant of a man, but with the gentlest of blue eyes. Colin was pretty sure Grace had a thing for him, the way she tightened up whenever their paths crossed, but she would rather die than admit it.

"So, seven o'clock tomorrow night, Evie?" Matt's smile was warm as Evie nodded.

As soon as he was out of earshot, Colin pounced, crowding her against the ambulance door.

"You nearly get yourself killed and now you have a date?"

"He asked me out to dinner. What's the big fucking deal?"

"The big fucking deal is that you ran into a burning house tonight, Evie! Do you know how stupid that was?"

"There wasn't time to wait for the cavalry!" Evie jerked the oxygen mask away from her face to glare at him without impediment. She was chewing a piece of gum, close enough that he could smell the mint on her breath.

"You could have waited." He was frustrated and unaware that he was holding her arms, his thumbs rubbing gentle circles into her soft skin.

"And your girlfriend could have burned to a crispy marshmallow by the time the firefighters arrived."

"She's not my girlfriend. Shit, that's not the point."

Their eyes were locked, and he saw her breath hitch as he raised one knuckle to trace the line of her jaw with the back of his fingers. *So soft.*

"I'm glad you're okay." He didn't mean to say that out loud.

"Me too." The words were whispered, and the slight tremble of her lush lower lip set off an answering tremor low in his gut. He leaned in. *Just a quick taste.*

Crash! The porch crumbled to the ground in a shower of sparks, and the pair leapt apart as Deirdre's wail rang out loud and clear over the chaos.

"I think you're being summoned," Evie murmured, arch.

"Don't drive home." Colin wagged a finger at her, shaken by the brief moment of insanity. The last thing either of them needed was the sexual zing that seemed impossible to ignore. He'd have to work harder at keeping his distance.

"Matt's going to give me a ride."

Colin ignored the lick of annoyance and nodded, then turned to join Deirdre, whose histrionics were quickly reaching impressive proportions. It was going to be a long night.

47

CHAPTER FIVE

EVIE THOUGHT SLEEP WOULD be
impossible, but for once, her body took over, exhaustion
and injury combining with a crash of adrenaline, and she
was out like a light the moment her head touched the
pillow. She slept for nearly twelve hours and woke to find
a host of new aches and bruises to accompany her healing
wounds. A hot shower and some ibuprofen took care of
most of the aches, and a cup of strong coffee dispelled the
morning cobwebs. Thus fortified, Evie looked around the
cabin – she should spend the day unpacking and cleaning,
using these last days before she started work to really get
settled and back up to full speed.

Ten minutes later she was in her car, making the
short drive to Deirdre's place, reasoning that she'd have
plenty of time to play house later.

Pulling up in the driveway, Evie was unsurprised
to see Tony, who was chatting with a young deputy with
shocking red hair, his badge pinned proudly to his shirt.
That must be Zeke, Evie supposed. He looked to be about
twenty, pale and a little jumpy.

She took in the charred remains of the house as
she stepped out of her car, and noted that a single fire
truck remained, parked behind Tony's jeep, emblazoned

with a Bright's Ferry Sheriff's Department logo. Luckily, Deirdre's red SUV was the only casualty from the night before, a victim of flaming debris, its roof crushed under a hefty chunk of burned wood.

Tony was impassive as he turned to face her.

"You're not inspiring me with a lot of confidence, Asher. No brownie points for nearly getting yourself killed before your first day."

"I assessed the situation and did what was necessary to protect a civilian life."

Tony folded his arms, grim.

"But you're right. I should have waited for backup," Evie conceded.

"Yes, you should have. That being said, your quick thinking saved Ms. Small's life. So why don't we call this one a draw, and you promise to keep the heroics to a minimum? They always lead to me filling out mountains of paperwork."

"I'll try to restrain myself." Evie grinned, and held out a hand to Zeke, who shook it vigorously.

"Nice to meet you, Miz Asher."

"Call me Evie."

"Zeke, why don't you go follow up with Deirdre, see if she has anything to add to her statement."

Zeke gulped.

"Yes, sir."

As he scurried away, Evie shook her head.

"She's going to eat him alive."

"The kid's got to toughen up. Besides, she's over at Colin's place. I'm sure he's got her under control."

The flare of irritation was unwelcome and disconcerting, and Evie turned to examine the soggy remains of the house.

"Did they figure out what started it?" she asked.

"Didn't I tell you to take a few days off?"

"I am!" Evie protested, but it was weak.

"Look, things are gonna get really busy around here in a couple of weeks during the Harvest Festival, and I'll need you at your fighting weight. You don't have anything to prove."

The words hung in the air between them. She *did* have something to prove. She had *everything* to prove – that she could start over in Bright's Ferry, that she was a good cop, that she could make up for the mistakes of her past. The longing that flooded her was almost palpable in the morning chill, and Tony must have felt it, because he sighed in resignation.

Evie pressed her advantage.

"Was it the boiler? Bad wiring?"

"Sure, if someone poured gasoline over the fuse box and set the wires on fire."

He led her around the side of the collapsed structure to indicate a couple of twisted metal gas cans. Evie crouched down to examine them.

"So it's arson. Too damaged for prints."

She wiped smudges of carbon on the back of her jeans.

"Does Deirdre have any enemies? Maybe there's a jealous wife who doesn't like her toying with her husband?"

Evie was proud of the fact that she managed to keep the snark out of her voice. Tony was shaking his head.

"Deirdre likes a good time, but she keeps her conquests single – married men aren't her style."

Shame filled Evie at the reminder that she was a living example of a homewrecker, albeit unintentionally. *Don't judge.*

"She's part-owner of a clothing shop on Main Street, pretty popular with the tourists, though my wife used to say the prices were insane." Tony cleared his throat and continued, "Maybe a firebug. I'll check in with the surrounding towns, see if they've had any similar incidents."

Evie nodded, her mind whirling with possibilities.

"Why don't you talk to her employees, see if they've noticed anything unusual, and then stop by the station. I'll need to get your statement, too. For the record."

He grinned, and the expression lit up his face – he really was eye-catching. Evie was relieved to feel nothing other than a basic appreciation for an attractive man. No more falling for the boss.

"We'll have you done in plenty of time for your date."

"Shit, does everyone know?" Evie groused.

"Like I said, word gets around."

"It's not even really a *date* date. He asked if I wanted to have dinner as a welcome to town sort of thing, and – "

"Asher, relax. Matt's a good guy. Go on, have fun."

"I'll try."

DEIRDRE'S SHOP ON MAIN was lovely, Evie had to admit, chock full of pretty, feminine things that made her realize that she spent most of her life in jeans, and actually had nothing to wear for her date tonight.

Not that it was a date. At least, she didn't *think* it was a date.

When Matt had asked her, his smile tentative and sweet, she had been inclined to say no, but he was nice and cute, and had just saved her life – one dinner couldn't hurt. Besides, he was humble, hard-working, and low key – the kind of guy she should be dating. Evie ignored the flash of wicked hazel eyes that popped into her head. From now on, nothing but wholesome, upstanding, ordinary men.

In Deirdre's shop, Evie questioned Jenny Bright and Susan Gunterson, a sweet long-time couple in their late sixties, and Deirdre's business partners, who were beside themselves that anyone would try to hurt Deirdre, but couldn't offer any new information. Yes, she was a bit spoiled, but the general consensus was that Deirdre was harmless.

Jenny was the great-great-granddaughter of Ellis Bright, the founding father, and the couple remembered Gram with great affection. Upon learning that Evie had saved Deirdre's life, they insisted on helping with her clothing dilemma, waving off her protests about gifts.

"If it bothers you, I'm sure we can find something in your price range," said Jenny, exchanging a look with Susan.

An hour later, Evie left the store with a short dress in shimmering blue, matching wisps of lingerie, and a pair of heels that all cost suspiciously less than Evie would have thought. She felt a little dazed. Once they got going, the two shop owners were forces of Nature, heaping dress after dress into her arms to try on in a whirlwind of fabric and helpful critique. Evie walked back to her car with advice about makeup and hair ringing in her ears.

By early afternoon, Evie was fading, and with no new findings, Tony sent her home with a strict admonishment to take a nap, already. For once, she had no desire to argue, and a few hours lounging on the couch in front of the fire did wonders.

After a quick shower, Evie took the time to blow her hair dry and apply a hint of makeup to cover the scrapes from last night's escapade. The whole ritual felt slightly unfamiliar – she'd never really had time for a boyfriend, and her relationship with Jack had been secret out of necessity. He'd spent more time impatiently peeling her out of her uniform than asking her to dress up.

She stood in front of the mirror, anxiously examining herself in the lace-edged silky strapless bra and tiny matching panties. Not that anyone would ever see them, but she had to admit that they were the most beautiful things she'd ever owned, even if they did show off a shocking amount of bare skin. Evie pulled the dress on and adjusted the miniscule straps, carefully draping a shawl around her shoulders to cover her bandaged shoulder. She tugged on the hem down, doubting that she could improve her reputation by flashing her ass at some unsuspecting patron over dinner, and then hurried to answer the knock on the door.

"Wow," Matt said, and the appreciation in his eyes went a long way toward soothing her nerves. He cleaned up nicely, but still gave off the impression of solid strength as he filled her doorway.

"Am I overdressed? I can change – "

"You look fantastic. Ready?"

She nodded and let him escort her to his SUV, opening the door for her.

A perfect gentleman, she thought. Maybe the evening would be a success after all.

The optimism lasted until the salad course. The restaurant was lively and crowded, a popular seafood place on the water, and Evie steered the conversation toward Matt, learning about the injuries that ruined his football dream but set him on the path toward life as a firefighter, his woodworking hobby, the charities he supported, and the house he was building himself. No politics, no troublesome relationships – just a nice, good-hearted man who seemed solid as a rock.

If I were smart, I'd fall for him.

As if on cue, the door opened and Colin entered with Deirdre. Evie was unprepared for the shock of reaction that landed in her stomach like a lodestone. She sipped her wine and tried not to notice how Colin's shoulders filled out his dark blazer, or the way Deirdre clutched his arm, her crimson nails matching the dress that was painted onto her voluptuous curves. Evie sipped her wine and wrenched her focus back to Matt, but he, too, was watching the couple move through the room like royalty. Colin smoothly stopped to shake hands with the locals while Deirdre enthusiastically accepted well-wishes after her near-tragedy.

"Poor Millie," said Matt.

"Hmmm?"

Matt nodded at a mousy waitress, pretty but unremarkable. She was watching Deirdre with barely-concealed hatred.

"Millicent Grayson. Her husband Bobby died a few months back, and it's no secret she's been trying to get Colin to pay her some attention. She and Deirdre really don't get along. Never have, not even back in high school."

"Really?" Evie examined the tense young woman with cop eyes, mentally adding her to a sparse list of potential suspects. But Matt was still talking.

"She's probably all bent out of shape because Deirdre's staying at Colin's until she finds another place."

"I can see why that might irk a woman who wants to romance the mayor." Evie squelched the uncomfortable prickle of jealousy that toyed with her insides.

Matt laughed.

"That's got to be most of the women in town. Half of them want to be First Lady of Bright's Ferry, the other half want his money."

"What money?"

"Didn't you know? Colin's rolling in it. He's like, some computer genius, made a bundle off a patent for a chip of some sort."

"Then what's he doing here?" Evie was baffled.

Matt shrugged and attacked his salad.

"Guess he wanted to come home."

Evie watched Colin help Deirdre into her chair, and saw her take the opportunity to trace a surreptitious finger up one muscled thigh as he moved away. Suddenly, she needed a little air.

"Do you mind? I'll be right back." She smiled at Matt, who stood as she did.

"Not at all. Take your time."

As she stood, Colin looked up, and their eyes met across the room. Evie felt nothing but heat as his shocked gaze slid downward, taking in her dress and every inch of bared skin. Feeling naked, she hurried blindly toward the hallway.

COLIN HAD NO IDEA what Deidre had been saying for the last three minutes, since all the blood in his brain had surged to his cock at the first sight of Evie in a silky, blue excuse for a dress that zapped his ability to focus on anything else. Mile-long legs, fabric that cupped her breasts and whispered down over her hips, held up by tiny blue straps that would be no match for his teeth. The silky ribbons of her hair teased the creamy perfection of her skin.

She'd dressed up for Matt, he realized, the thought a surprising irritation. He tried to block it out, but as Deirdre chattered away, already focused on new plans for her damaged property, Colin was bombarded with upsetting images – the big firefighter escorting Evie to the doorway of her grandmother's cabin, winding her glorious dark hair around his fist while he took her mouth, tracing the curves of her breasts as he pulled her dress down, and worst of all, Evie's gray eyes darkening with lust as she pulled him inside, her nimble fingers eagerly working on his buttons. *Fuck.*

The room suddenly felt very hot.

"You don't look so good, sweetie," Deirdre suddenly noticed, arching one perfect eyebrow, "Want some water?"

"Go ahead and order for me," Colin said, patting her hand, "I'll be right back."

The hallway leading to the restrooms was more of a long glassed-in patio overlooking the wharf, with a small curtained room at the far end, usually reserved for private romantic dinners.

Colin came around the corner and stopped short as Evie came out of the Ladies' Room, looking tense. Her eyes widened. Colin couldn't catch his breath, and fumbled to think of something important to say. He'd spent a tedious day with Deirdre, who had taken the fire as a sign that they should move in together, and wouldn't listen to reason, already coming up with massive plans to redecorate his parents' house. All the while, Colin worried about Evie, trying desperately to remember why he wanted to stay away from her in the first place.

"Hello, there."

"Hi."

He was planning to say something relevant, to ask her if Tony had figured out what started the fire, but one second they were staring at each other, and the next he was propelling her back toward the empty alcove room, behind the red velvet curtains, and pressing her against the rich damask wall, the light low and intimate.

"This isn't a good idea, Colin," she whispered, her eyes huge.

Colin knew she was probably right, but the heat of her body under the thin silk, the softness of her breasts yielding to his muscular strength as he pinned her against the wall, clouded his mind.

Bad, bad, bad, Daniels.

He was trying to convince himself to let her go before this got even more out of hand when she took the decision away from him, stretching up to capture his mouth in a kiss so carnal and hot that any second thoughts melted away like butter on a hot griddle.

EVIE HAD NO DOUBT that kissing Colin was a terrible idea, nor that it was entirely her fault. She could have asked him to let her go or pushed him away, but the strength of his body against hers felt criminally good, and the now-familiar scent of his aftershave was driving her crazy, and that annoying, sexy mouth was *right there*. All of her good intentions vanished as she moved, and her mouth met his in a hot, wet tangle, battling for control, the taste of him addictive. *So good.*

They were relatively concealed in the alcove, the muted sounds of the restaurant no more than a pleasant buzz behind them, and Evie's breath hitched as Colin pulled slightly away to ease the shawl off her shoulders while he nibbled her lower lip. She shivered as he traced the straps of her dress, easing the one on her good shoulder away as his lips started a slow path down her throat and his hands settled on her ribcage, carefully avoiding her injuries, his thumbs lightly caressing the underside of her breasts.

"Nice dress, Miss Asher," he murmured.

"It's new." Evie's head fell back as Colin sucked gently at the sensitive spot where neck met shoulder, and she slid her hands under his blazer, learning the ridges of his torso through the soft material of his shirt. Suddenly, the only thing that mattered was getting her hands on all that warm muscled flesh, and she was shocked to find herself tugging the material free from his jeans. When her greedy hands burrowed beneath, exploring the contours of his body, reveling in the heat that poured off of him, Colin groaned and wrapped his arms around her, pulling her back in for another drugging kiss.

The shift pressed his rigid cock against her lower stomach, and she wrenched her mouth away, gasping. He felt huge, and her empty pussy clenched, already damp for him.

"God, Evie, feel what you do to me?"

In an effortless move that made her whole body tighten with need, he lifted her, pressing her against the wall again and sliding one muscular leg between hers, forcing her to ride his thigh, pushing her skirt up. The solid muscle rubbed her swollen clit deliciously as he rolled his hips, the bulge of his erection against her abdomen. Colin licked a spot under her jaw and Evie moaned, her nails digging into his back under his shirt as he started a steady rocking motion that was designed to dissolve her whole body into a puddle on the floor in no time.

With a naughty grin Evie felt rather than saw, Colin slid a hand between them, tracing the lacy edge of her barely-there panties.

"Bet these are pretty, too," he murmured.

His fingers grazed her soft flesh as he tugged the damp panel to the side, and she jerked.

"What are you – oh, *God* – "

Without the soft silk as a barrier, the rough denim of his jeans rasped directly against her wet pussy, firing nerve endings and sending shards of pleasure ripping through her as he rocked, and rocked, and rocked. Evie whimpered and he swallowed the sound.

"You're burning me alive," he muttered, cupping her ass under her skirt to haul her even closer, rub harder, taking her mouth with his like a conqueror.

Evie had completely lost control of the situation, a fact that terrified her, but the way he handled her body felt shockingly good, the practiced thrusts of his tongue and hips and the hard cock between them a delicious preview of the sexual delight he had to offer. She felt tension coiling in her abdomen, in her pussy, as he nipped her lower lip.

"That's right, baby," he groaned, "let me give you what you need."

The words splashed over Evie like icy water, dousing her desire, and with a monumental effort that had her shoulder and side protesting, she shoved him away. Colin stared at her, rumpled and aroused and panting, the heat in his eyes enough to make her knees buckle, but she was too shaken and angry to care.

"You don't have a fucking clue what I need."

Trembling, she straightened her dress.

"Evie, what the hell – "

"This was a mistake."

"It was just a kiss. Is that such a big deal?" The harsh rasp of his voice belied the flippant words, but Evie didn't notice as she hurriedly retrieved her shawl, which had fallen to the floor.

"It's a big deal when you toy with people's feelings. It's a big deal when you tell a girl that you want her and then spend the night with someone else. It's a huge deal when you make your girlfriend believe you love her, when you make promises, but really you're just fucking around on your wife, ruining lives and careers for the sake of your dick, Jack."

Evie stared at him, horrified as the angry words spilled out of her mouth, almost involuntarily, and the play of emotion on Colin's face moved from confusion to grim realization to sympathy.

"I think you're confusing me with someone else," he said gently, and placed a hand on her arm.

She jerked away as though she'd been stung. What a complete disaster.

I'm sorry, she wanted to say, but the words got stuck, and the only thing she could manage was a shocked, "Oh God – " before she hurried away.

Back at the table, Matt was waiting for her with a smile that faded as he took in her agitated state.

"You look rattled. What's the matter?"

Evie dredged up a shaky smile.

"Nothing, just a little headache. Do you mind if we cut our evening short? I'm so sorry."

Ever courteous, Matt paid the bill and escorted her out, admonishing himself for not realizing that a date might be too much after last night's near miss. At her doorstep, he kissed her cheek in brotherly fashion.

"I hope we can try again sometime soon."

Evie didn't have the heart to tell him that given her taste in men, she was *this close* to just swearing them off entirely, and agreed to a rain check. Inside the house, she stripped off the fancy new duds, poured a glass of wine, and climbed into a scalding bubble bath, refusing to think about Colin and fuming over the fact Jack Forrest was still ruining her life from hundreds of miles away.

THE SLUT HADN'T BEEN injured in the fire, not a mark on that putrid white skin. The new deputy had saved her, not knowing what she was. She'd walked in with Matt Harris. He was a good boy – he deserved someone upstanding, like the deputy. Meanwhile, the restaurant was crowded, and while Colin was in the restroom, the slut had chatted up the men at the next table, flirting and leaning in to give them a glimpse of the ample cleavage exposed by her whorish red gown.

She was supposed to burn, the cleansing fire stripping away the cloak of false beauty to reveal the ugliness of lust and sin beneath. That she lived was an affront. That Colin seemed determined to offer solace in his bed was worse. Colin's judgment was impaired. He wasn't thinking clearly, or he'd see her for what she really was.

He needed direction.

Guidance.

Discipline.

He returned from the restroom, smiling as Deirdre handed him a glass of wine, but the unease in his face was apparent. Clearly he sensed the decay that lay under her smooth lips and bright blue eyes.

A little punishment would show him the difference between right and wrong. That's what correction was for. It was for his own good.

CHAPTER SIX

COLIN TOSSED AND TURNED in the dark, unable to get comfortable. He'd made it through dinner, but Deirdre's less than subtle attempts to undress him as they drove back to the house were aggressive and annoying. He caught a glimpse of Evie's cabin, light glowing softly in the darkness across the hill, and realized that he couldn't sleep with Deirdre tonight. Even though she hadn't been talking about him, Evie's lecture still hit home, and for the first time in quite a while, Colin couldn't stomach the thought of fun between the sheets without meaning or repercussion. Deirdre had not been pleased to be bundled into the guest room, but an hour later, the house was quiet, and Colin was alone with his thoughts.

Unfortunately, they were all of Evie.

Trouble or no, Colin was fascinated with the town's new addition, and now that he'd held her against him, tasted her lips and the vanilla spice of her skin, all he wanted to do was peel that silky blue dress down for a better look at those lacy bits of nothing she was wearing tonight, and then wrap those gorgeous legs around him and feel her surrender to his desire as he filled her to bursting with his aching cock.

Like that was ever going to happen.

Colin was beginning to put the pieces together, although there were gaps. The woman was tough as nails on the outside, the result of a horrific childhood with an alcoholic father, but some married asshole named "Jack" had found a way around the armor to the sweetness that Colin had gotten a heady taste of tonight. However, instead of treasuring it, nurturing it, he'd seduced and humiliated her, leaving her with zero trust in men and a chip on her shoulder the size of Nantucket. She was better off without him, no doubt about it.

Not that Colin was the man for the job, either, he assured himself. The concept of commitment sent a chill through his veins. And if he were going to tie himself to one woman, Evie was the exact opposite of the sweetly submissive type he preferred. Still, the thought of some other jerk getting intimately acquainted with Evie's softness was like a thorn in his paw.

Matt could be over there right now.

Colin groaned and tried to banish the idea from his mind, but then the image became one of *him* instead, and he slid a hand down to take firm hold of his dick, which surged to attention as the pictures flooded his brain – Evie's fingers tunneling through his hair to hold him close while he sampled those perfect tits, begging for release while he lapped up the nectar between her thighs, and obediently sinking to her knees at his request, eagerly taking his dick into her mouth.

Oh God, this won't take long.

He came with a harsh moan, pleasure racing through his system. Afterward, Colin lay panting, his come cooling on his skin as the usual sense of satisfaction warred with frustration.

The woman was going to drive him crazy. He realized he was halfway there when he came to the conclusion that the only way to get Evie Asher out of his mind might be to fuck her out of his system. For that to happen, he would probably have to get her to trust him enough to let him close enough to slide between those pretty thighs. For *that* miracle to occur, he was going to have to actually date her, at least for a while. As in a real relationship, until the fascination wore off. Which might take months, given his inability to stop thinking about her. Wasn't *that* a scary thought?

A quick trip to the adjoining bathroom cleaned away the evidence of his desire, but the unease remained.

Moonlight spilled through the window and as Colin headed back to bed, a flash of movement outside caught his eye.

Something was out there.

He hesitated – in town it wasn't unusual to get raccoons and possums, and the occasional deer, but up here in the hills, there was the chance of a run-in with larger predators – a coyote or even the rare mountain lion. Still, something didn't feel right. It didn't *feel* like an animal. It felt like a person, someone watching the house.

Knowing he was probably just overreacting, Colin pulled on some clothes and grabbed a baseball bat from the closet.

Just a quick look around.

In the dark, he found sneakers and padded downstairs, careful not to wake Deirdre as he opened the front door and stepped onto the porch.

Quiet.

Colin peered into the dark, sure he'd seen *something*.

A rustle from half-completed construction on the side of the house had him jumping out of his skin, his heart pounding. He raised the bat, edging closer to where a loose tarp flapped in the chill night breeze.

Nothing.

Colin peered around the scaffolding, but everything was as it should be – dark and empty, with materials piled up neatly, waiting for the workmen to return next week for the next stage of the project.

He felt the blow a split second before the shocking pain in his head, and then the ground was tilting up to meet him. Throwing a useless arm out, he caught the edge of a workbench, sending boxes of nails and tools clattering to the ground as the world went black.

Somewhere in the distance, Colin heard footsteps and then Deirdre's high-pitched scream.

"Oh my God, Colin!"

And then *nothing.*

EVIE WAS LYING ON a beach. Sun, sand, and a shirtless Colin rubbing sunscreen into her back on a tropical island. He had the best hands, warm and big and sure as they massaged the creamy lotion into her skin. He growled approvingly as he untied her bikini top to cup her breasts from behind, which was okay because they had the beach all to themselves. He pinched and rolled her oh-so-sensitive nipples while he whispered into her ear all the hot and dirty things he was planning to do to her.

Then they were naked, and she was pushing him back to the sand. He went willingly, obediently holding his large cock steady for her as she sank down, breathlessly taking him to the hilt. She smiled as he let her fuck him any way she wanted to, giving up control to just accept all the pleasure she could give him.

If only someone would stop that damned bell from ringing, everything would be perfect.

Evie pried bleary eyes open, her skin tight, her pussy throbbing, unsatisfied as reality came rushing back. She reached for her phone, glancing at the clock – twelve-thirty AM.

"Asher. Hey, Tony."

Thirty seconds later she was racing around the room, finding clothes and keys, and then out the door and into her car, wrenching the little sedan down the road to the fork and then up toward the Daniels house. She was shocked to find her hands were trembling as she jumped out of the car and hurried up to bang on the front door.

The handsome young Latino man who opened the door was barely out of college, but carried himself with the poise of someone much older. Still, he looked puzzled to see a harried woman on the stoop. Evie flashed her badge and tried to look professional, because that's what a cop did when summoned to a crime scene in the middle of the night. The young man's expression cleared, and he stepped aside to let her in.

"You must be Deputy Asher. Tom Castillo, Colin's assistant."

Evie shook hands and glanced over at the living room, where Deirdre was nursing a very large glass of scotch from an armchair, wrapped in a blanket. Colin sat on the couch while Jocelyn, in flannel cat-printed PJs with a jacket flung over them, was gently examining his eyes as he held an ice pack to the back of his head. Evie felt the hard knot of worry uncoil ever so slightly.

"Hey, Doc," she said, stepping into the room.

Colin watched her warily as she approached.

Well, of course he's wary. You basically let all the crazy out. Now he wouldn't come near you with a ten-foot pole. Despite her ongoing resolution to avoid him at all costs, the thought was supremely depressing.

"Tony sent me. I was closest."

Colin didn't look happy about that, either. Jocelyn sat back.

"You might have a slight concussion, but you're lucky that head of yours is so damned hard, Colin. With great reluctance, I'm going to let you stay here for the night."

She grabbed a notepad from her bag and scrawled a quick list.

"You notice any of these symptoms, do not hesitate, do not drive. Call me, call Tom. Have someone get you to the ER."

Evie cleared her throat.

"I know it's late, but I have to ask a few questions while the incident is still fresh in your mind."

Colin sighed.

"I saw something move outside, I came out to check it out, got about ten steps off the porch, and then the bastard brained me with a two by four. That's about it."

Evie turned to Deirdre.

"Why did you come outside, Ms. Small?"

Deirdre gulped her drink, and Jocelyn and Evie exchanged a look.

"Well, I heard the most awful clatter."

She paused.

"When I fell, I knocked over the workbench," Colin offered.

"Yes," said Deirdre, "that was it. Then I came outside and saw Colin lying unconscious, and so I called Tom. He must have been alone because he came right over."

She giggled, hiccupped, and then frowned.

Tom rolled his eyes.

"Colin had already come around when I got here, but I thought the Doc should have a look at him just in case."

"You thought right," agreed Jocelyn, packing her bag again.

"Was anything disturbed?" Evie asked, turning back to Colin, forcing herself to hold his gaze.

"No."

"Anything taken?"

"No."

"We can't really rule out a burglar. You may have interrupted him or her before they had a chance to break in."

"I keep telling you, this isn't New York. Besides, why would someone come all the way up here when all the tourist traps in town are there for the taking?"

Evie hesitated, and then voiced what was really on her mind.

"It seems to be common knowledge that Ms. Small was staying here tonight. After the fire last night, it's possible that she was the target."

Colin frowned.

"I thought the fire was an accident."

"Signs point to arson."

The four looked to Deirdre, but she was out like a light, curled up in the armchair, cuddling her glass.

"I'll put her to bed," said Tom, moving the glass, and then lifting her into his arms in a surprising show of lean strength.

"Thanks, Tom," said Colin, and Evie bit her lip, trying not to ask whose bed Tom was planning to put her in. She wasn't used to this kind of jealousy, and didn't like it. But the harder she tried to ignore it, the more it sank green claws into her stomach. There was something between them, whether it she acknowledged it or not.

"Best not to mention this to anyone in town," remarked Colin, "Candace will freak, and Dreyer will immediately make it a reason to oust me from office. Until we know what's going on, let's keep it between us."

Tom disappeared upstairs with Deirdre, and Evie turned to go.

"I need to take a look outside," Evie said, and Colin got up from the couch.

"You're not going alone."

"I have a gun. You have a concussion."

"I don't care."

They glared at each other until Jocelyn breezed past them toward the door.

"Someone can walk me to my car. Colin, I'll stop by tomorrow."

Evie fumed as Colin smirked and hurried to escort the good doctor outside. She watched from the porch as Jocelyn drove away, and then flicked on the flashlight on her keychain.

"What do you think you're going to find out here?"

"I don't know. That's why I'm looking. Quit crowding me." Evie elbowed Colin in the ribs and he fell back a step, quiet as she examined the gravel, the driveway, and the discarded two by four near the addition to the house.

"Think you'll get any prints off of that?" Colin asked.

"The wood is pretty rough, but we can try." Evie grabbed a roll of plastic sheeting that was leaning against a wall and used her keys to cut a large swath, carefully wrapping the wood to protect any evidence. She packed it away in her trunk and resumed her exploration, all the while aware of Colin's eyes on her.

"How long have you been a cop?" he asked.

"A few years."

"Ever deal with an arson case?"

"Once. A drug dealer set a rival's walk-up on fire."

"You don't really think someone's trying to kill Deirdre, do you? Who would do that?"

Evie turned on him, shining the light into his face.

"I don't know, do you?"

"What?"

"I just got here. I don't know anyone. You're the town's golden boy, so you tell me – who has it out for your girlfriend? Did she screw someone over?"

Her voice was harsher than she meant it to be, and Colin scowled down at her. Abruptly, Evie lowered the flashlight.

"As far as I know, Evie doesn't have any real enemies. At least nobody that would burn down her house or try to actually harm her."

He paused, scanning her face in the moonlight.

"Evie," he said gently, "I didn't sleep with her tonight."

"It's none of my business," Evie asserted, but swallowed the sudden lump in her throat as she hurried toward the addition to the house.

Colin didn't comment, but followed.

They found the animal laid out on a workbench. Ripped to bloody shreds, it might have been a raccoon or a badger at one point, but it was impossible to tell. There was no mistaking it for an attack by another animal, because scrawled in blood next to the remains of the poor creature was a single word. *Sin.*

"It's a terrible prank," said Colin, though he sounded unconvinced.

"This is far beyond a prank," said Evie, "Someone's trying to kill your girlfriend." And she whipped out her phone to call Tony, swiftly explaining the situation.

Colin argued with her as she photographed the crime scene with her camera phone. He argued with her as Zeke appeared to take the night watch, and he argued with her as she climbed back into her car.

"It just doesn't make sense," he insisted.

"Crazy doesn't have to make sense," she retorted. "You'd better get to bed. It's late and I'm sure Deirdre is getting cold."

And she shut the door.

"Wait a minute."

Evie didn't wait, but took off, arriving at the cabin a few minutes later. She didn't want to argue anymore, she didn't want to prove a point. All she wanted was to catch a few hours of sleep and tackle this whole mess in the morning. The parting jibe had been thoughtless, but she was cranky and annoyed, both with Colin and herself.

A spurt of gravel and Evie looked up, surprised, as Colin's truck skidded to a halt behind her car. He jumped out and slammed the door behind him, stalking up to the porch, where she hadn't even had a chance to get her key in the lock.

"You think you've got me all figured out," he said, "I'm just a spoiled rich kid who grew up to be mayor of a small town where everyone kisses my ass and the women fall at my feet, is that right?"

"I think you have no idea how dangerous the world can be, and you live in secluded little bubble."

Evie squeaked as Colin grabbed her and hauled her close.

"Maybe I've managed to keep my nose clean, but that doesn't mean I think the world is all sunshine and gumdrops. And yes, I've had a series of casual relationships, but that doesn't mean that whatever this is between us hasn't knocked me on my ass, same as you. And if I have to say it a thousand times, I will. I did *not* sleep with Deirdre tonight, and I doubt I'm going to any time in the foreseeable future."

Don't ask don't ask don't ask.

"Why not?"

Evie cursed internally, but strained to read the answer in his face in the dim glow of Gram's porch light.

I don't want to know.

She really wanted to know.

The answer was so simple, so stunning, and so utterly delicious as he lowered his mouth to hers, not in the frenzied carnal encounter from earlier, but in a kiss so sweet and seductive that Evie moaned into his mouth.

Colin deftly unsnapped her holster and set her weapon down on the porch railing, never losing contact with her lips, his tongue stroking hers, hot and wet, demanding a response with every deft lick.

She was barely aware of the move as he eased her down to sit on the porch swing and knelt on the porch between her legs, pulling her pussy snugly against his torso. Evie held him tight, exploring the muscles of his shoulders, pulling her mouth away to taste the hard edge of his jawline and then cruise back to find his lips. She managed to pull herself out of the sensual stupor when she felt him undoing the buttons of the shirt under her open jacket. Evie pushed on his shoulder.

"We're outside."

"Mmm-hmmm." Colin kissed the skin he exposed at the base of her throat as he undid another button.

"Colin, I don't know about this."

"I do."

CHAPTER SEVEN

EVIE WASN'T WEARING A bra. The discovery made Colin feel like cheering, and he wondered how he could have missed such an important piece of information when she stomped over earlier that night. It must be the blow to the head, he reasoned as he pulled the edges of her shirt back to expose the creamy mounds. Round and plump, and crested with perfectly shaped nipples. Colin's mouth watered.

Evie had gone still under his hands, clearly trying to decide whether to flee or stay.

Oh stay, baby.

Colin leaned forward to nuzzle a path between the generous globes. He had a real thing for breasts, and while Deirdre's were impressive in a structured, manmade way, Evie's tits were full and soft and the very best that Mother Nature had to offer. He licked his lips, his cock already pounding behind the zipper of his jeans.

She pushed at his shoulder again, but it was less of a push and more of a caress, and then he felt the bite of her nails as he sucked one luscious berry-shaped nipple into his mouth.

"Colin!" she gasped.

He didn't answer, but words were beyond him anyway. Her nipple was velvety smooth in his mouth, swollen and sweet as he laved and suckled, plumping and kneading her other breast in his hand, his head full of the heady scent of Evie and the vanilla lotion she used.

Her fingers threaded through his hair, rasping erotically against his scalp, careful to avoid the tender lump. Colin pulled back slightly, wishing he could make out the color of her nipples in the soft glow of the porch light, but it was too dark. He could see that they were drawn up tight, whether from the cold or his mouth he didn't know. He licked one, nipping it lightly with his teeth, savoring the hitch in her breath.

"So sensitive. Think I could make you come just by sucking your tits?"

"I don't – " She couldn't finish the thought, and he grinned against her breast, sliding a hand into the dip at the back of her jeans, caressing the small of her back and lower, to the very top of the sweet cleft that separated the cheeks of her ass. She shivered.

Her pussy was pressed tightly against him, the heat of her meltingly good even through her jeans.

With a last leisurely flick of his tongue against her nipples, Colin started kissing his way down her torso.

"We shouldn't be doing this out here." She sounded nervous, as though she had just remembered that though there wasn't anyone around for miles, she was half-naked on her front porch, letting him play with her bare breasts.

I wonder what else you'll let me do, thought Colin, and he murmured, "I want to taste you."

She tensed against him, froze as he undid the button on her jeans. For a moment he thought she might pull away, so he slowed down, nuzzling her navel and the delicate skin under the open waistband. She relaxed a fraction and he let out a breath, and then made sure she was watching as he gripped the zipper of her jeans in his teeth and slowly drew it down.

"Seriously? That's one of your moves?" she choked out, and her voice was amused but gratifyingly breathless, "What, do you moonlight as a gigolo in your spare time?"

"Would you hire me?"

She snorted in derision as he yanked her jeans to her ankles and settled between her knees again, noting that she'd switched the lacy little things for another pair of bikini panties, white in the darkness.

"You'd make a terrible gigolo. You always have to be in charge."

"Says the woman who agonizes over anyone ever doing anything for her, ever."

"There's nothing wrong with being independent."

"There's nothing wrong with letting someone take care of you once in a while, either."

"It's none of your business."

They glared at each other.

"Fuck it," he snarled, and surged forward to capture her mouth in a brutal clash of teeth and lips, his tongue in her mouth, his frustration rolling over him in waves. She gasped into his mouth when he grabbed a handful of her panties and jerked, the material shredding like paper.

She was tense and angry, and Colin wanted her soft and yielding, giving him everything he wanted. He hadn't realized how her stubbornness would push his buttons, turning his natural urge to be in control into something hot and driving. He wanted her to surrender, to let him pile the pleasure on any way he wanted to until they were both drowning in it.

Slow, he ordered himself.

He kept his fingers gentle as he learned her pussy for the first time, his anger melting away, no match for the wet heat and delightful surprises he discovered with light strokes of his fingertips – the small patch of soft hair at the top of her mound, the delicate bare folds, and the sweet bud of her clit, already swollen for him.

His cock was going to tear free of its confinement and strangle him, but he would make this good for her, he vowed. It was already *spectacular* for him. Colin swallowed her whimper and then tore his lips away to trace a path down her throat as he tested her opening, teasing but not entering with one slick finger, while the scent of her made his mouth water.

"I'm going to lick you, right here. You're going to let me, aren't you?"

Arousal made him hoarse, but he forced himself to wait for her response, though heat coursed through his veins like wildfire.

Evie gave up all at once, her fingers digging into his shoulders, clinging as though she couldn't help herself. The ghost of her lips against his temple set off a small quake in the vicinity of his heart. Evie had a sweet side, though she tried like hell to hide it.

Colin pushed her knees wider, his hands splayed on her thighs, and used his thumbs to expose her core. Although her plump folds were in shadow, he caught the glimmer of wetness in the soft glow of the porch light.

"Hell, yeah," he muttered, and lowered his head for a taste.

THIS ISN'T HAPPENING, THOUGHT Evie. There was no way she was letting Colin Daniels eat her out on the front porch of Gram's house, bare and spread for him, the squirrels, and God knows what other woodland creatures were watching. All it took was one hot, wet lick and her rational brain went away, along with any inhibitions that would prevent her from accepting any and all sexual pleasure he wanted to give her. Evie didn't like it, not one bit. She was independent, she was in control, she was –

Oh God, right there.

His tongue did something to her clit that had her crying out, arching her pussy into his mouth. Colin chuckled, *infuriating man*, and did it again, this time sliding two long fingers into her sheath in a move so carnal she whimpered.

"That's right, baby," he crooned against the pad of her pussy, "Give me everything. Mmm…tight and wet."

He expertly finger-fucked her until she was writhing for him, unable to hold back the little sounds that were shocking to her ears, but that he seemed to enjoy as he nibbled gently on her engorged clit. He pulled his digits out, only to replace them with his tongue. A hot, mind-blowing lash of his tongue at her core made good on his promise, and then he closed his mouth over her, using the pad of one slick forefinger to rub diabolical circles into her hungry clit while he sucked and thrust with delicate precision.

Evie didn't want to think about *how* he got to be so good with his mouth, but all that practice paid off because one second she was straining against him, sure she couldn't stand it one moment longer, and the next, all that lovely tension burst and she was melting over him like oozing honey, a sharp cry of surprise pulled from her throat.

You never came like that *for Jack*, she noted.

Evie was too replete to let the realization do more than drift through her consciousness, and besides, Colin was still between her thighs, gently lapping as her tremors subsided.

"Next time, I'm going to feel this sweet pussy come apart around my cock."

The jolt of pleasure at the rough words had her hips jerking involuntarily. He chuckled softly and placed a gentle kiss at the very top of her cleft, and then rested his cheek against her abdomen while her racing heart finally started to calm. The rasp of stubble from his jaw on her tender flesh sent a new wave of shivers through her body.

Evie leaned back against the porch swing and hesitantly stroked Colin's cheek as he propped his chin on her belly, his hazel eyes nearly glowing with heat and arousal and male satisfaction at her response to him.

"Do you want to come in?" she whispered, knowing that despite their intensely erotic interlude out here on the porch, the invitation represented a much bigger step, and the beginnings of trust. She squashed the nerves and worries about the future and focused on what she wanted in the moment – Colin's big naked body moving against her, driving her to peak again and again with his hands and mouth and cock. She licked her lips, waiting for his answer.

It never came, because at that moment, the porch light *exploded* above them in a shower of sparks and glass.

"Down!"

Evie reacted without thinking, tackling Colin to the ground and dragging him under the relative cover of the swing. She yanked up her jeans and hastily buttoned her shirt.

"Are you hurt?" she demanded, running her hands over him, checking for wounds.

"I'm fine. Is someone shooting at us?" He sounded shocked.

CRACK!

Another shot rang out, and splinters of wood rained down on their heads. Evie scrambled up, fumbling for her weapon on the railing, but Colin yanked her back down.

"What the hell do you think you're doing?"

"I've already been shot twice this year, I'm not going to let it happen again! Do something useful and call for help!"

Ignoring his grasping hands, she pushed to her hands and knees as the gunfire continued, destroying one of Gram's planters, followed by one of the front windows.

CRACK! CRACK!

The shooter had made a mistake in taking out the light, and Evie took advantage of the darkness to find her weapon, getting it out and up in a matter of seconds to return fire. For a minute they traded shots, but it was like shooting into a black hole – the night was dark as pitch, and the dense trees around her property offered too much cover. They were pinned down, and the best Evie could do was hold the shooter off until help arrived or the bastard ran out of ammo. She could hear Colin whispering urgently into his cell phone, but her senses were focused on the woods – every snap of a twig, every rustle of branches.

Suddenly, the gunfire ceased, and Evie strained to hear the slightest sound from her position by the railing.

"He's making a run for it," she muttered, and started to slither down the stairs, but Colin grabbed her around the waist and hauled her back.

"Are you out of your mind? You're not chasing down some lunatic with a gun in the dark."

"He's getting away!" Evie protested, though she knew he was right. Her first instinct was to go after their assailant while the getting was good, almost immediately followed by the inner cop slapping her upside the head.

Protect the civilian, protect yourself. A few weeks off the beat and you've forgotten everything, Asher.

"He could be waiting behind a tree for you to stumble out, guns blazing. Just stay put. Zeke will be here in two minutes."

"Fine. I know." She was tense, keeping her eyes peeled and her gun trained on the darkness, trying in vain to catch a glimpse of a criminal who more than likely was no longer there.

Colin kept his arms around her, as though to reassure himself that she wasn't going to bolt off the porch and get herself killed, and she had to admit that the strength of his body behind hers was reassuring.

The flash of headlights coming up the hill send a flood of relief running through Evie, and she relaxed minutely as Zeke pulled his truck into the driveway. Zeke clambered out of the truck, his freckled face stark white and scared in the glow of the two powerful flashlights. A quick sweep of the trees proved what Evie already suspected – the shooter was long gone.

"Anybody hurt?" he called.

Cautiously, Evie untangled herself from Colin's grip and edged out to meet him.

"We're okay."

More lights, and Tony's SUV jerked up the last stretch of hill, screeching to a halt. He stepped out, clearly pissed, as Colin moved to examine a bullet hole in the side of his truck.

"Dammit," he muttered.

"Zeke, take Colin and make sure the house is secure. Asher, you're with me." Tony's voice was clipped and angry.

Evie couldn't bear to look at Colin, but nodded, taking one of Zeke's flashlights and hurrying after Tony into the trees. A few minutes of searching led to a pile of 9mm shell casings and a few muddy boot prints, too smudged to be of any use.

Tony insisted on a careful grid search of the whole area, and Evie was impressed by the small town sheriff's efficiency and attention to detail. She made a mental note to do some digging into Sheriff Arnetto – the man was as layered as an onion, and played everything close to the vest.

They were finishing the sweep of the grounds when Tony finally turned to her.

"The fire, the dead animal, the attack on Colin, and now this."

His eyes were steady on hers as the truth hit home. Evie sucked in a breath and leaned against Tony's truck, working it out.

"So, Deirdre's not the target. At least not directly. He's after Colin."

"But he didn't kill him when he had the chance. He just knocked him out," noted Tony, "because he's sending a message. Remember the blood? Sin. It's a stalker."

Evie forced an incredulous laugh, not wanting to believe it, but her stomach sank.

"Don't fuck the mayor, or else?"

"Colin's a great guy, but he hasn't exactly been living like a monk since he moved back to town. Hell hath no fury, right?"

Colin stepped out on the porch, followed by Zeke.

"The house is secure," squeaked the young deputy, importantly.

"Colin, I'm going to need a list of every woman you've hooked up with since you came back to Bright's Ferry. And the ones in Boston, too." Tony's voice was matter-of-fact, as though it were an everyday request.

Colin sputtered for a moment, and then, "What the hell, Tony?"

Evie spoke up, keeping her voice as professional as she could manage, ticking off her fingers as she ran down the list.

"Deirdre's car got keyed the other day, probably while she was with you. The next day, her house burns to the ground. Instead of staying away from Deirdre, which is what the attacker seems to want, everyone in town sees the happy couple at the restaurant tonight – "

Evie paused to clear her throat, glad that Colin couldn't see her expression in the glare of the flashlights.

"Later, Deirdre spends the night at your house. Enraged, the attacker leaves a dead animal and a message, and then knocks you out when you nearly catch her in the act."

She stopped, the rest of the list stuck, but Tony smoothly picked up the narrative.

"The attacker sticks around to make sure you're not seriously injured, and then follows you back here. Whatever she saw sends her flying into a rage, and here we are."

Evie's face heated as Tony deliberately kept his voice bland and nonjudgmental. If the attacker was really watching, they would have gotten an eyeful.

For a hot second, the memory of Colin's tongue expertly flicking her clit while his fingers slid inside her with slow, deliberate thrusts, intruded, and Evie felt dizzy. She quickly shook it off – not the time or the place, not that her pussy seemed to care. Her clit throbbed like a toothache.

It must be the adrenaline, she thought. She hoped.

Colin leaned down to swipe a piece of white fabric from the porch, which he casually slipped into his pocket. *Her panties*. Evie stifled a groan.

"Colin," said Tony, deadly serious, "You've got a stalker."

"That's ridiculous," Colin retorted, "completely – wait."

"What?" asked Evie as Colin froze.

"There have been letters. To the office. Really twisted stuff."

"And you didn't report them? Shit, Daniels." Tony was pissed.

Colin paced the driveway, running his fingers through his hair, agitated.

"Look, hate mail is part of the job. Few times a year we get someone railing about anarchy and all that nonsense. The only reason I remember these is that they really rattled Candace. I figured they were just from some nutjob trying to let off a little steam."

"We need to see those letters."

Colin nodded, sitting down on the front steps, trying to process everything.

"Uh, Sheriff?" Zeke's voice was hesitant in the darkness.

"Yeah, Zeke?"

"Well, the stalker doesn't necessarily have to be one of Mr. Daniels'…uh…girlfriends. It could just be someone that wants to make us think that. Or someone jealous."

"That's a good point," said Evie, "Anyone who dislikes Colin, doesn't think he's fit to be mayor, anyone holding a grudge…"

Colin was shaking his head.

"I can't believe this. So, what happens now?"

"Unfortunately, Evie seems to have caught the stalker's attention. We don't want to antagonize him or her by seeing you two together, but at the same time, I don't have the manpower to have someone keep a separate eye on you, Deirdre, and Evie, too."

"I can take care of myself," Evie insisted.

"That's not a good idea," growled Colin, "and besides, I was nowhere near Deirdre when that maniac set her house on fire."

"True enough."

Tony kicked at the gravel, considering their options.

"For tonight, Asher, go bunk down at the Daniels' house. Zeke, you take the night watch and I'll see if I can't drum up some volunteers from the Fire Department to join you. Tomorrow, we'll go through those letters and try to figure out who this lunatic is before someone really gets hurt. Until he or she is caught, no one goes anywhere alone."

Spending the night on Colin's couch while he and Deirdre slept upstairs sounded like punishment to Evie, but she nodded. At least this way she could keep him safe.

The drive back to Colin's house was short, and as Evie followed his truck, she could see Zeke's headlights in the rearview mirror. She yawned, drained from the emotional highs and lows of the evening along with the stress of two near-death experiences in two days' time.

An hour ago, Evie had been completely focused on the idea of stripping Colin out of his clothes and satisfying the lust that had plagued her from the moment she'd seen him, half-naked in his doorway. Now, all she wanted was a good night's sleep without any surprises, gunshots, or blood. Sexual satisfaction was all well and good, but her shoulder and side were stiff, throbbing dully, reminding her that she needed to take something, that she really wasn't yet up to speed.

She pulled up behind him in the driveway and hoped that he was as tired as she was – she felt raw, and wasn't ready for another confrontation. Colin got out of the truck and started toward her, but suddenly the front door opened and Tom stumbled out, his eyes wide with shock, blood on his hands and shirt.

"Colin, it's Deirdre – she's dead."

CHAPTER EIGHT

THE WHOLE TOWN TURNED out for Deirdre's funeral two days later. She may have had a reputation, but she was one of Bright's Ferry's own, and the community was horrified and saddened by her abrupt and brutal death.

In the small cemetery overlooking the bay, Colin stood over the gravesite with Jenny Bright and Susan Gunterson, who wept openly next to Deirdre's parents as the preacher performed the service. From the corner of his eye, he could see Evie standing with Tony at the edge of the crowd, not listening but watching instead, taking in the expressions and reactions of his friends and neighbors with her sharp gray eyes.

It bothered him, the idea that someone he knew and cared for had most probably done this – the crimes were too personal to be a random killer passing through, but the rational conclusion was almost impossible to believe. It bothered him more that he seemed to be at the center of the killer's focus, and as a result, the people in his life were now in danger.

He stared down at Deirdre's coffin as it was lowered into the ground, thinking about the loss of a beautiful, fun-loving woman, overwhelmed by guilt.

The blood on Tom's hands and clothes had been Deirdre's. As he explained it later, he'd been in the living room when he heard the gunshot, and raced upstairs to find the hall window open and Deirdre lying in a pool of blood in the guest room. Tom was nearly incoherent as he explained how he tried to revive her, but Evie gently assured him that there was nothing he could do. Her voice was softer and more soothing than Colin had ever heard it.

Colin sent Tom home with strict instructions to rest, and then Tony arrived, and the whole search process had begun all over again. It was a long, grueling night, and by the time the EMTs had taken Deirdre's body, and Tony had left Zeke and a volunteer firefighter built like a truck to guard the house, the sky was already starting to lighten.

Colin took one look at Evie, swaying with exhaustion, and swept her off her feet, carrying her upstairs to lay her down in his bed. She protested, of course, but was asleep before he even got her shoes off. He removed her jacket, but left the rest of her clothing on, remembering with vivid clarity that she had nothing on underneath the jeans and light shirt.

If he were a better man, he admitted to himself, he would have taken the couch. Instead, Colin climbed into bed behind her and pulled her back to his chest, relieved and gratified when she murmured softly and snuggled back against him, her ass nestling perfectly against his groin, her hands clutching his arm between her breasts, the softness of her hair at his mouth. After the shock and stress of the night, the living warmth of her body against his felt like Heaven, but he only had a moment to savor it before sinking into sleep like a stone.

When he woke, she was gone.

Colin hadn't seen her since, and he, Tom, and Candace were underwater at the office as the rumors started to fly and the panicked community demanded answers. Yesterday, Tony had marched in to confiscate the hate mailbox, and Colin had managed to pry small bits of information from him – the gun that shot at them was the same one used to kill Deirdre.

Evie had basically moved in down at the Sheriff's Department, catnapping in the town's one holding cell for a few hours at a time in between taking statements from every woman on Colin's list, cataloguing and labeling every scrap of evidence.

The grief and anger over Deirdre's death was momentarily swamped by sheer horror as he imagined what the woman who held his fascination was uncovering by interrogating all the women he'd pursued over the past couple of years.

God, if she was wary about me before…

AS THE CROWD DISPERSED, offering their condolences to Deirdre's parents and tossing flowers into the grave as they passed, Evie watched carefully, noting who lingered, who hurried away, who fidgeted during the ceremony, and who wept. But she was distracted, her gaze moving back to Colin again and again.

He was grave and pale, his hazel eyes filled with emotion, gorgeous in a black suit, and Evie felt a low hum of hostility as women approached to hug him and press their cheeks against his, offering comfort and perhaps more. Some were blatant about it, some less so, but Evie found she was getting good at figuring out which of Bright's Ferry's female residents were just friends, and which were dying to jump Colin Daniels' finely-sculpted bones.

Evie watched Grace give Colin's hand a sympathetic squeeze, and then was surprised when the young woman, her purple hair artfully pulled back into an elaborate braid, smiled at her and headed in her direction.

"I just wanted to make sure you were okay. Crazy couple of days, huh?"

"It's not what I expected when I decided to move back here, that's for sure."

Grace considered her with clear brown eyes, and Evie felt like squirming.

"Why don't you stop by the library later? We can grab some lunch and you can fill me in."

"I can't really talk about the case – "

"Not about that. I want hear all about how you managed to turn Colin inside out."

Evie started to protest, but Grace laughed.

"Don't bother. I've known him since the third grade, and he's never been as rattled by anyone as he is by you."

"I'm not sleeping with him," Evie blurted out. *Not technically, anyway.*

"Maybe you should start." Grace's eyes twinkled, "From what I hear, it's quite the earth-shattering experience. Not that I would know firsthand, of course. Too much of a big brother, little sister vibe there."

She wrinkled her nose and Evie's mouth stretched in an answering grin.

"But seriously," Grace asked, sobering, "Is he in danger? I keep hearing rumors about stalkers and serial killers. Some people are even saying that Deirdre committed suicide because Colin wouldn't marry her, which is nonsense. I know it's a horrible thing to say, but the woman thought way too much of herself to deliberately deprive the men of Bright's Ferry of her presence. If there is someone out there – someone that might hurt Colin – "

"I'm not going to let that happen. I promise."

Impulsively, Grace hugged her, and a surprised Evie hugged back.

"I know you won't," Grace whispered.

Evie watched her go, her long black skirts catching the breeze.

"She likes you."

Colin's voice at her elbow had her stumbling back, startled. Smoothly, he caught her arm to steady her, and a warm tremor snaked through her at the brush of his skin.

"You should take that as a compliment," Colin continued, "She doesn't make friends easily."

"I know the feeling."

Colin took a step closer, into her personal space, and lowered his voice to something warm and intimate.

"You disappeared on me the other day."

"I'm trying to catch a killer."

"I don't want you putting yourself in danger."

Evie noticed belatedly that he hadn't let go of her arm, and was rubbing a gentle circle on the inside of her wrist that threatened to crumble her defenses.

She barely remembered him taking her to bed after the hours searching the house and the grounds for evidence, but she definitely remembered waking up. The feeling of his arms around her, his solid strength at her back, and the warmth of his breath on her neck was delicious, and she spent a few decadent minutes watching him sleep, the sun streaming through the windows, painting his skin gold. One soft kiss pressed to the corner of his mouth had him stirring, but he didn't wake as she untangled herself and sneaked out.

If he had woken to find her soft and vulnerable, she wasn't sure she'd have been able to resist the heat in his eyes or those elegant hands peeling her clothing off and pressing her into the mattress…and that would make today so much harder.

She pulled her arm away and he frowned.

"Colin, it isn't safe for us to be talking like this."

"You're saying I can't have a conversation with a woman without painting a target on her back? I'm not going to let some freak hold me hostage."

Evie kept her voice low, though she really wanted to shout at him, her temper rising.

"Not every woman, just the women you fuck!"

"I haven't fucked you yet," he breathed, "although we came damned close."

Evie fought the blush that was working its way up her face.

"That's for the best."

"The hell it is. Shit, I knew it was a bad idea to give you that list. Not a single one of those women is capable of murder, and now you've got this image of me as – as – " He sputtered, unable to come up with a term shocking enough.

"As a horny tomcat with a fear of commitment?" The barb was delivered in a dulcet tone, and Colin glared at her.

"I don't care if you sleep with half the women in Massachusetts," *And Heaven forgive me* for that lie, "but the stalker does. Those letters aren't just full of hate, Colin. They're warnings to shape up, to repent, to make up for all the immoral fucking around you do because you're rich and popular and have a great ass." Her voice was growing louder.

"Why don't I get right on that?" Colin was fuming now. "I never slept with anyone who didn't totally understand how the cards were dealt, and I'm not going to apologize for enjoying the hell out of each and every one of them before we parted ways. Amicably, I might add. And if you're going to lecture me on immorality, why don't we lay out your relationship history and do a little side by side comparison?"

Evie slapped him. She couldn't help it. He looked as stunned as she felt, and though the cemetery was mostly empty now, the few that lingered got a good look. Evie was sure that they'd be fueling the gossip mill at the local watering holes within an hour.

She let her hand drop, clenching her fist.

"I'm sorry. I shouldn't have done that."

He was breathing hard, but he nodded.

"I'm sorry, too. This is why I try to keep all my relationships casual, but God, Evie, you just push all my buttons."

"You're distracting me when I need to focus on keeping you safe and on stopping that lunatic out there. Besides, I can't get involved. I just can't."

Not again.

Colin blew out a frustrated breath.

"This whole situation is driving me batty. Deirdre's been murdered. I can't go anywhere without a police escort. And this thing between us isn't doing either of us any good right now. So let's table it until the stalker is caught. Truce?"

"Truce. It's just as well," she said, with a small smile, "Casual isn't my thing."

"COLIN! COLIN DANIELS. I need a word." The voice was imperious and unfortunately, very familiar.

Colin looked up to see Dreyer Morton hurrying up the hill, his gold-tipped walking cane gouging holes in the cemetery turf. He didn't actually need it, but carried it anyway, a not-so-subtle reminder to the community that he was a wealthy man. A *very* wealthy man who owned a piece of half the businesses in town. The middle-aged black man was frowning, as usual, and for the millionth time, Colin wondered how a man so successful could find so many petty little things to be unhappy about.

"Good afternoon, Dreyer. I didn't realize that you and Deirdre were acquainted. How kind of you to come pay your respects." Colin was all smooth politeness.

Dreyer glared at him before turning to the grave that two workmen were busily filling in. Ignoring them, he folded his hands over his cane and tipped his head down respectfully. After a moment, he muttered, "Amen," and turned back to them, a scowl on his face.

"Despite her unfortunate promiscuity, Deirdre Small had roots in this community that went back for generations. No parent should have to bury a child, no matter what kind of a disappointment they turn out to be. May the poor girl rest in peace."

"I'll pass your kind words along to her parents." Colin was having trouble keeping his tone even, but Dreyer seemed oblivious. He spared Evie a quick glance, dismissing her almost immediately as being beneath his notice.

"Was there something I could do for you, Dreyer?"

"I want to know why you're permitting the Sheriff's Department to question Althea. She doesn't know anything about this foul business."

Colin groaned internally, but some wickedly amused inner demon pushed him to point at Evie.

"Why don't you ask them yourself? Dreyer, have you met Bright's Ferry's newest deputy? Dreyer Morton, Evie Asher."

Evie gave him a look that could cut glass, but stepped forward, holding out a hand. Dreyer ignored it, and Colin could see her biting her lip as she adjusted, pulling on the cop demeanor with ease.

"Mr. Morton, we're questioning anyone who may have a connection to Mr. Daniels, no matter how small."

"If that's the case, you may as well line up the entire population of Bright's Ferry. For God's sake, he's the mayor. But leave my daughter out of it."

Dreyer towered over Evie, but she stood her ground, her back ramrod straight.

"We have reason to believe that these…incidents…may have something to do with Mr. Daniels' romantic entanglements. Your daughter had a brief relationship with Mr. Daniels last year, so we just needed to get her statement."

"What she had, Deputy Asher, was a brief moment of insanity. Otherwise, she would never have embarked on an adulterous affair with a known womanizer half her age."

"Careful, Dreyer." Colin had long since learned to ignore most of Dreyer's blather, but there was a limit. "First of all, it's none of your business. Secondly, Althea and I had a short, mutually satisfying relationship shortly after her divorce and then parted ways. That's all."

Dreyer looked like he was about to blow a gasket.

"The divorce was a mistake. She would have gone back to her husband if you hadn't been there to seduce her away."

Colin could feel Evie's eyes on him, fascinated, as he shook his head in disbelief.

"You're deluding yourself, Dreyer. That rich asshole you pushed her to marry had a mistress in Boston for years. What do you think all of those business trips were about? Besides, she's remarried now, and as far as I can tell, blissfully happy."

"Married to a man who can't possibly give her or my granddaughters the life they deserve," Dreyer snapped, getting in Colin's face. Colin refused to back down.

"You're a snob, Dreyer. Cal is a good man. He may not be a corporate hack – "

"He works in a hardware store!"

"He's a small business owner!"

Evie cleared her throat.

Colin got a grip on his temper. Much as he wanted to ram that gold-tipped cane down Dreyer's throat, physical violence wouldn't help the situation.

"Your daughter is a grown woman. Her choices in life are exactly that. *Her* choices."

"When it comes to my daughter being accused of murder, young man, I have a parental duty to protect her interests."

Evie tried, once more, for diplomacy.

"No one has accused your daughter of anything, Mr. Morton. We're in the early stages of trying to find out what happened so that we can prevent it from happening again."

"I'll tell you how to prevent it from happening again. Keep him," and he pointed the sharp end of his cane toward Colin, "away from my Althea. And the same goes for you."

Evie stiffened, as Dreyer sneered at her.

"Oh yes, don't think I don't know who you are. Your grandmother was a pillar of the community. Her only mistake was in letting her daughter run off with that no account boy. Laura Asher was stubborn, and too independent for her own good. If your grandfather were alive, he never would have permitted it to happen."

Colin expected bloodshed from Evie as the vile, judgmental drivel spewed from Dreyer's mouth. What he didn't expect was the shattered look in her eyes, and the way she seemed to shrink into herself. He realized with a shock that she wasn't going to defend herself or her family. But, of course, Dreyer wasn't done.

"And it seems that the apple doesn't fall far from the tree. I have friends in New York, Miss Asher. No wonder you've become a target for this so-called stalker. He's clearly seeking out women with loose morals, the kind that wreck homes and ruin lives. You have experience in that area, don't you?"

"Dreyer, that's enough."

"I think the town has a right to know what kind of woman is policing their streets, Mr. Daniels."

Colin forgot that he was supposed to be playing peacemaker and grabbed the older man by the lapels.

"If you breathe one word to anyone, I will personally take this cane and shove it so far up your ass – "

"Colin, stop."

Evie's quiet voice, grave and calm, broke through the red haze clouding his vision. Dreyer squirmed in his grasp and Colin dropped him. Shakily straightening his jacket, Dreyer aimed poisoned glares at both of them.

"I'm just protecting my own. Althea was a good girl until Colin came back to town."

"She's still a good woman. And I may not have been in love with her, but I liked her. I've always liked her. I respect her enormously."

Dreyer scoffed, "You don't know the meaning of the word."

He started to march away, but Evie suddenly snapped out of her daze.

"Where were you Monday night?"

She hurried after him, blocking his path down the hill.

"My private life is none of your business, young lady."

"It's a simple question." Evie's voice was like ice.

"And if I choose not to answer it?"

"Then we'll have to talk down at the station. I'm sure you don't want that."

"Unless you're charging me with something, Miss Asher, get out of my way. This constitutes harassment, and I assure you that you'll be hearing from my lawyer," he sputtered, and Colin was amused to see him shaken by Evie's cool glare.

"Why would you need a lawyer? Have you done something illegal? Tell him I'll be expecting his call. We're going to sit down and have a chat, Mr. Morton, with or without legal counsel. Your call."

Not giving him a chance to respond, she marched back toward Colin. For a moment it looked as if Dreyer would storm back to confront her, but he simply stomped down the hill, stabbing the ground as he went, muttering darkly under his breath.

For the first time all day, Colin felt like smiling.

"I want to kiss you so badly right now."

He didn't miss the little flare of heat in her eyes, but she lowered long lashes.

"Well, restrain yourself." Her voice was prim.

But it thrilled him to the core as she darted a quick look up at him. And smiled.

CHAPTER NINE

SOMETIMES THIS JOB REALLY, really sucks, thought Evie as she stepped out of the Sheriff's Department into the square after a long morning of interviews.

Preparations for the upcoming Harvest Festival were already in full swing, and a bandstand was going up, along with rows of tents and a dance floor. The carnival rides were still in pieces, waiting to be put together, but already a crowd of eager kids had gathered near the roped-off area, puzzling out which gears and beams belonged to which carnival deathtrap, and which should be avoided on a stomach full of cotton candy and popcorn.

Evie watched the fun, wistful – she'd never had a gaggle of friends like that. Her father put her to work cooking and cleaning for him from the moment she was tall enough to reach the stove or handle a broom. At least there was school, where she could be around other kids her own age, but she was shy and awkward, and never wanted to explain her family situation. As a result, Evie had had a Cinderella-esque childhood, minus the Prince Charming or the magic pumpkins – school dances were skipped to make dinner for Dad, boyfriends were avoided for their own protection. Dad often couldn't tell the difference between her and her late mother, and Evie always tried to avoid his alcohol-soaked rages, with varying degrees of success. She had quickly realized that she would have to be her own fairy godmother, and the moment she graduated from her city college, she applied to the Police Academy.

But there had never been the kind of fun for fun's sake that seemed to shimmer in the air in Bright's Ferry, and Evie longed to be a part of it. She wanted to escort the local kids through the scary corn maze, gorge herself sick on cider and apple pie, and dance with a cute guy who would hold her close and whisper how pretty she looked under the lights of the Harvest Dance. Hot hazel eyes flashed into her mind and she frowned.

She did *not* want to try to figure out which one of her new neighbors was a killer.

And she *really* did not want to fall under the spell of Bright's Ferry's boy toy mayor.

The last couple of days of interviews had given her a clearer picture of Colin. He worked hard, he played hard, but was almost always gone by morning. Tender and compassionate, but unwilling to let a relationship go further than friendship. A sexual force between the sheets. All of the women agreed on *that* point – Colin had plenty to offer a woman, and knew exactly how to offer it. He liked to be in charge – *no surprise there* – and women were putty in his hands.

Evie had asked practical questions of the eight women she questioned – *How long were you together? Was the relationship sexual in nature? Did anyone get hurt when it ended? Where were you the night of the murder?* Through each interview, Evie attempted to keep her tone calm and professional, trying to ignore the irrelevant pieces of information she picked up as the women recounted their flings with Colin, with little success. *Magnetically attractive?* Check. *Sex god?* Check. *Body to make the angels weep?* Double check.

It was humiliating to note how similar her reactions were to those of Colin's bevy of former girlfriends. Her stomach fluttered as she took note of the one major difference – all of her close encounters with Colin had been intense. No casual friendship. No easygoing, fun-filled sexual romps. *What does it mean?* She thought about the way he'd pleasured her, driving her upward with hands and mouth as though he would never stop.

Enough, Evie, the inner cop bitched, *stop thinking about him dragging you behind the gazebo to have his wicked way with you and deal with the situation at hand. Hello, killer?*

Evie started toward Town Hall, sifting through the various interviews and pieces of information of the last few days. The problem was that there were too many suspects, and not enough at the same time. None of the women Colin had dated seemed to bear him any ill will, although that would be easy to conceal. Dreyer Morton was a possibility, but Evie accepted the fact that being a total asshole didn't necessarily make him a killer.

Millicent Grayson is next on my list. Unfortunately, the mousy little waitress was proving difficult to track down. A stop at the restaurant had revealed that she'd been home caring for her sick toddler, but she hadn't returned any of the messages Evie or Tony had left for her over the last couple of days.

There were two options – they could either wait for the stalker to strike again and hope to find more evidence to point them in the right direction, or they could cast the net wider and hope for a break in the case. Given that Evie seemed to be directly in the path of danger, she was putting her efforts into the second option. Besides, she wasn't going to sit around and wait for some deranged lunatic to put a bullet in her skull because he or she was under the mistaken impression that Evie and Colin were a couple. Evie firmly banished the thought of Colin's mouth on her skin and started up the steps of Town Hall.

Sometimes this job totally sucks, she thought again, sighing. There were still two people to interview from her initial list, and Evie had a feeling that Colin was going to be a tad bit upset.

"WOW, YOUR OFFICE IS so swanky."

Colin looked up to see Evie lounging in the doorway, admiring the high ceiling and polished antique furniture that hadn't been upgraded in a century. As always, his pulse jumped at the sight of her.

"Makes me look like a grownup, right? I've got them all fooled." He smiled and gestured toward a chair.

Shutting the door behind her, Evie returned his grin and sprawled in the visitor's chair across the desk.

"I hear you're a computer genius."

Colin leaned back, getting comfortable. He knew that there was no way this was a social call, but if he could steal a few minutes of casual conversation with Evie before she dropped whatever bomb she was planning to ruin his day with, he would take it. *Pathetic, man*, he scolded himself, but without heat. The funeral that morning had been difficult, and it was refreshing to sit across from Evie without arguments, without accusations, in the relative safety of his office – since the attacks, Tony had the place guarded like Fort Knox.

"I dabble."

"I dabble in baking and make a decent strawberry rhubarb pie. You dabble in computer technology and make millions. You could be running a company somewhere." A note of disbelief crept into her voice, and Colin waved a hand dismissively.

"I thought about it. But then Mom and Dad died, and I came home to sort things out. After a few weeks I realized that I liked everyone knowing my name, and having a town full of quirky little traditions. So I stayed."

"Do you still do the computer stuff?"

Colin shrugged, self-conscious.

"Sometimes. It pays well, and…I kind of like being a geek."

Evie burst out laughing as he felt heat creeping up his neck.

"I promise I won't tell," she teased.

"On another note," Colin leaned forward across the desk, his voice low and suggestive, "I'd love to taste your strawberry rhubarb pie."

There it is, he thought, as a punch of heat hit low and sparks seemed to arc between them.

Until her eyes went sad and dark.

"How would that work?" Evie asked softly, "We'd have a few nights together, maybe a few weeks. Everywhere we'd go, I'd hear them thinking, there goes Laura Asher's daughter, what a shame. Her father was a philandering drunk and her mother killed three people. Oh, and did you hear? She was fucking her boss. Makes sense, since she's currently fucking the mayor. And after a while, you'd lose interest and move on."

"You don't think much of me. Or yourself." he gritted out.

Evie shook her head.

"I can't be another fling, Colin."

"It wouldn't be like that."

Her eyes widened as the words hung between them.

"Don't make promises," she urged, "We're all acting on stress and adrenaline right now. I want us to be friends when this is over."

"I don't think we can just be friends, Evie." He thought of her coming apart against his mouth, the soft weight of her breast in his hand.

"That's the only offer on the table, Mr. Daniels."

They stared at each other for a long moment. Colin could feel the frustration churning inside him. On a purely intellectual level, he knew she was right – "relationship" wasn't exactly a term he'd embraced in the past. But he knew one thing – he wanted her. Badly enough to consider locking the door so he could lay her on his desk and suckle her sweet tits until she was begging him to fuck her. Badly enough to risk courting her, stalker or no stalker. Badly enough to actually think about what a real relationship might be like.

Sure, they fought like cats and dogs, but he'd seen her with Grace, watched as she comforted a grief-stricken Tom. Evie was damaged and suspicious, but so damned sweet under the tough and capable cop that his teeth ached. He was dying for another taste of her, and she wanted that, too, whether she was willing to admit it or not. But until she was ready to budge even the tiniest bit –

"Was there something you needed, Deputy?"

EVIE FLINCHED AT THE cool tone, but reminded herself that it was for the best. The man was a distraction, and although there hadn't been an incident in two days, Evie couldn't relax – the stalker was still out there, waiting. There wasn't any time to waste on relationships that were doomed before they even got started.

"I need to talk to Tom and Candace."

"About security? They're being careful. I had Tony put a detail on – "

"Not about security."

Evie saw the realization hit home and braced herself.

"Are you out of your fucking mind?!?"

His voice was loud enough that Evie was surprised that the windows stayed intact. Colin stood up, unable to keep his seat as the fury bubbled over.

"Candace and Tom had nothing to do with any of this!"

"I'm just covering all my bases."

A timid knock on the door.

"Go away!" Colin yelled. He turned on Evie, seething. "You don't know them the way I do – they keep this office and my life running. Candace worked for my father, for God's sake. She used to babysit me! And I'd trust Tom with my life."

Evie was out of her chair and in his face before she even realized that she was moving.

"Do you get that someone has a sick obsession with you? Every woman you touch is a threat. Every person you talk to is in danger. The stalker is someone close to you, Colin. Someone you see all the time, maybe someone you've had sex with. You have to take this seriously!"

Colin paced, and Evie could see him struggling with her brutal words.

"They're my friends."

He leaned against the window frame, staring out at the main square.

"I know," Evie said, her voice softening unintentionally, "but there's somebody in this town who thinks that the way you live your life is an abomination, who wants you to think and act in a manner they've prescribed. And when you don't follow that ridiculous, impossible set of invisible directions – "

"People get hurt," Colin finished.

"People get hurt." Evie echoed.

She joined him by the window.

"I want my world back," he murmured.

"Then let me do my job," said Evie.

For a moment, he just looked at her, and her stomach fluttered as he raised a hand to cup her cheek, his skin warm and slightly rough against her.

"Don't – " she whispered.

"So touchy," he teased. The ghost of fingers traced her lips and she had an insane desire to suck one into her mouth, to savor the salt of his skin. His hand dropped and he sighed.

"Come on, let's get this over with."

Ten minutes later Evie was sitting at Colin's desk across from a cool and collected Candace Wilkinson, while Colin pouted in the adjoining chair.

"You shouldn't be in here," Evie noted sternly, and watched Colin set his jaw.

"It's my office, and there isn't anything you have to say to her that you can't say to me."

Evie calculated the odds of getting Colin to leave her to question his employees in peace and threw up her hands in resignation.

"Fine, but no interruptions."

Insolently, Colin "zipped" his mouth closed and adopted the air of an angelic choir boy.

Fighting the urge to roll her eyes, Evie turned her attention to Candace.

"Mrs. Wilkinson – "

"Just call her Candace."

Evie glared at Colin, who subsided back against his chair. She raised an eyebrow at the severe woman sitting across from her, and Candace nodded. There was something off-putting about someone that neat, thought Evie. Her brown hair was smooth with just a hint of gray, her shirt pressed and smoothly tucked into a blue plaid skirt. Every move was economical and efficient. And her light blue eyes had a look of steel that Evie knew all too well. The woman would have made a great cop.

"So, Candace. How long have you worked for this office?"

"Since Hank Daniels stepped in, twenty-five years ago."

"That's a long time."

Candace smiled, but it didn't reach her eyes. "You find something you excel at and you stick with it, Miss Asher."

"Deputy Asher."

Candace smiled in apology. "Deputy Asher, of course."

"Can you tell me where you were Monday night?"

Evie ignored Colin's restless movements.

"I was in my car. Alan's prescription was filled by the pharmacy across the bay by mistake."

"Jocelyn doesn't usually make those kinds of mistakes." Colin frowned.

"Yes, well, she's had more on her plate than usual. At her age, she really shouldn't be making house calls at all hours."

Candace smiled again, but Evie felt the sting – the last house call the good doctor had made before the murder was hers. She felt the pull of her wounded side as she shifted in her chair.

"I suppose the pharmacy can confirm that."

"Of course, dear."

"Are we done?" Colin sounded aggravated.

"You are free to leave anytime you want." Evie pointed out, waspish.

Sheesh, if the temperature in here goes down any further, I'm going to need a parka.

Between Candace's ice maiden routine and Colin taking every question personally, the weather in the Mayor's office was feeling decidedly chilly.

"Candace, can you think of any reason someone might want to harm Colin?"

"Everyone loves Colin." Candace frowned for the first time. "Everyone loved his father, too. Bright's Ferry has been lucky to have such fine, upstanding men to lead the way."

Colin managed to look self-conscious, and Candace noticed.

"Now Colin, you need to learn to take a compliment. You've done a wonderful job and you know it. Alan and I are very proud of you."

"What about Colin's former girlfriends? Did any of them express any sort of unhappiness or anger after the relationship was over?"

Evie could feel the icicles growing on her insides as Colin glowered, but the question had to be asked.

"Not that I can think of. Although Millicent Grayson was not terribly happy to see him with Deirdre. Really, Colin, what were you thinking, taking her to that restaurant?"

Colin sunk into his chair, chastened.

"I've never dated Millicent Grayson," he muttered.

Interesting. Evie pressed onward.

"Just a couple more questions, and we'll be done here."

Candace cocked her head and considered Evie.

"I remember your mother. We were in school together. You look just like her."

Evie swallowed hard, but forced a smile.

"Can you tell me about the letters? How did they arrive?"

Candace frowned, looking uncomfortable for the first time.

"They've always been slipped under the door when I arrive on Mondays."

"And you're the first one here?"

"Yes."

"Video cameras? Alarm system?" Evie asked, looking to Colin, who shook his head.

"It's on the To Do list, but the wiring in the building can barely keep the lights running. You might think I'm the most popular guy in town, but watch what happens when I try to request additional funds from the Town Council for an upgrade. Ever seen an angry mob?" Colin grinned ruefully.

"Security guards?"

"Crime has never really been a problem in Bright's Ferry," offered Candace reprovingly, "At least, not until recently."

She pursed her lips with a pointed look at Evie.

"The building is locked up at the end of the day," Colin added hastily, "and only a handful of people have keys. But the idea that one of them is the culprit – "

Evie sighed, scrubbing her hands down her face.

"I really need to have Tony give you a lesson in basic security. I realize Bright's Ferry is a tiny speck on the map, but this isn't the 1950s, and even if there weren't some crazy psycho out there, break-ins happen all the time. I could pick the main lock downstairs with a pen and a pair of tweezers."

"Thank you for that expert opinion." Candace's voice was frosty. "If that's all, I do have work to do."

Evie nodded.

"I may have some follow up questions for you, but that's it for now."

Candace got up to leave, contempt apparent in every line of her frame, but Evie's voice had her turning back.

"Candace, please keep in mind that my only goal here is to keep Colin and the rest of the town safe from harm. There is someone out there, and we're all in danger. I really wish the members of this community would remember that and start cooperating."

Candace stared her down.

"You're an outsider, Deputy, even if you are an Asher. The people of Bright's Ferry don't appreciate outsiders poking their noses where they're not wanted and accusing the neighbors of obsession and murder. Whoever did this is clearly not one of us."

With that, she flounced out, leaving Evie with a scowling Colin.

"Satisfied?" he asked, petulant, "She had nothing to do with it."

"I need to call the pharmacy and confirm her whereabouts."

"You don't let up, do you?"

Evie could feel another argument brewing, but she didn't care.

"How about this? Why don't you make a list of everyone you know for a fact is not the killer? How many people would be on that list, Colin? Ten? A hundred? More?"

Colin was silent, fuming, and Evie leaned her hands on the desk, locking eyes as she made her point.

"The sooner you learn that none of these people are really who they say they are, the better. Underneath the surface of one of these good, hardworking citizens is someone who mutilated a poor animal and left it as a message, who shot at us from the woods, who emptied a clip into Deirdre Small. Until that person is caught, you can't trust anyone!"

"Is that how you get by?" Colin asked, "Assuming that everyone is hiding something? Pushing everyone away so that you run no risk of getting hurt? There are people you can count on in this world if you just let them in."

"This from the man who refuses to date a woman long enough to learn more than her name and cup size."

They were nose to nose now, furious.

Evie was horrified to feel unexpected tears welling up, and hastily swallowed them as his eyes widened.

"Don't go anywhere without an escort," she ordered, and fled.

CHAPTER TEN

"WANT ANOTHER ONE?" GRACE asked as Evie slurped up the dregs of one of Mary's famous cherry shakes in the corner booth of the diner.

"Keep 'em coming." Evie muttered, and Grace signaled a waitress.

"Must be serious. Or are you one of those people who can suck down carbs and not regret it in the morning?" Fiona Morton's brown eyes brimmed with amusement as she twirled a forkful of salad.

After the confrontation with Colin, Evie stormed out of the building, forgetting that she still needed to question Tom. Ten minutes of aimless wandering and Evie had her temper under control, and was surprised to find herself just a few steps away from Bright's Ferry's lone library. Remembering that she had promised Grace that she would stop by, she headed inside. Grace greeted her effusively, and Evie was once again bemused by the contrast between the librarian's perky personality and her dramatic Goth look. Grace insisted on giving her the tour, and Evie was impressed by the scope of the little library's collection. Clearly the library was something Grace was passionate about, and Evie felt a little pang of emotion as she filled out an application for a library card.

Like a normal Bright's Ferry resident.

"You look like you need a drink," Grace had noted astutely, and dragged her through the stacks in search of Fiona. Upon introducing her to the young woman with the beautiful mocha skin and slim figure, Evie was surprised to find that she was Dreyer Morton's granddaughter, just out of college – a sweet and even-tempered young woman with a wry sense of humor. The girl was easily persuaded to take a long lunch, and a few minutes later they were tucked into their "regular" booth in the back corner.

When Mary set a luscious pink cherry shake in front of Evie, all thoughts of a double shot of tequila vanished into an overload of sweet, creamy goodness. Grace's eyes widened as Evie downed the first shake in a matter of moments, while a waitress came around with a tray full of chicken salads.

Evie took a deep breath and pushed the empty glass away.

"So, spill. What did Colin do now?" Grace asked.

"Nothing. Everything. He just refuses to accept that someone he knows is guilty, and it's getting in the way of my investigation."

"Colin needs to fix things. It's hard for him to step back and let someone else take the lead."

"Yeah, I got the total control freak vibe right off the bat."

Fiona laughed, but Grace only grinned into her salad.

"That's because you two are exactly, precisely alike."

"I think I'm insulted," said Evie, but she shrunk into her seat.

"Come on, Evie, you know it's true. And as for Colin's…let's call it popularity…with the women in this town – the last thing Colin wants is for anyone to get hurt.

Including himself, so he doesn't get too involved. Sound familiar?"

"Maybe a little." Evie stabbed a fork into her salad.

For a moment, they chewed in silence, as Evie stewed over Grace's perceptive comments. *Maybe a lot,* she thought, *The difference is that I don't sleep with everything that moves. No, I just don't get involved at all, because look at what happens when I do. God, Asher, maybe you should take a page from his book and just get laid. No emotions, no sweet words or promises.*

"Well, this table got really serious all of a sudden," said Fiona, and leaned over for a sip of Evie's second shake, which had just arrived at the table. "Mmm…don't let me have any more of that. Hey, Evie, I heard you had a date with Matt Harris."

She waggled her eyebrows suggestively. If Evie hadn't been watching, she would have missed Grace's almost imperceptible stiffening across the table.

"It wasn't really a date. Just dinner."

"If I had a hot firefighter interested in me, I wouldn't settle for just dinner." Fiona shivered delicately.

"You're single, right?" Evie remarked, "Why don't you ask him out?"

"Because my grandfather would have a heart attack." Fiona scowled, "He's still pissed that I went to Boston to go to college instead of up here, so I'm trying not to antagonize him."

"Why come back at all?"

Fiona laughed.

"Haven't you noticed? There's something about this place. Besides, a certain violet-haired librarian offered me a job."

She good-naturedly elbowed Grace in the ribs.

"So for the moment I am single and, sadly, celibate. But Gracie here could stand to see a little action. But she thinks Matt is too nice."

"He *is* too nice." Grace grumbled.

"The man is smart, funny, polite, kind to animals, and built like a freaking sexual beast, Gracie, and the way he looks at you is in no way *nice*." Fiona insisted, but Grace shook her head.

"Look, we're not compatible, okay? He needs a nice wholesome girl with normal tastes. Can we just drop it, please?"

Fiona shrugged and reached for Evie's shake again.

"Do you mind?"

"Go for it," said Evie absently, wondering about the puzzle that was Grace. She was a study in contradictions – sweet and bubbly, but with a love for the dark and spooky and Goth. And if she read between the lines, Evie would hazard a guess that she was looking for someone with slightly darker sexual preferences than a wholesome blond firefighter could provide. But she kept this thought to herself. Despite the frustrations of the morning, having lunch with "the girls" was a new experience for Evie, and she was determined to nurture these friendships.

"Do you – " she began, hesitant, "Do you two want to come over for dinner next week? I know you're busy with the Harvest Festival, and we're all kind of at DEFCON One, but I thought it might be nice…"

"I'll bring the wine," said Fiona immediately, "And Grace will make brownies, because she has a way with chocolate that would bring a grown man to his knees. Maybe you should make a batch for Matt Harris, Gracie. One bite and I'll bet all those nice, *wholesome* tendencies would go right out the window."

Gracie frowned and threw a balled-up napkin at her friend, whose eyes were twinkling.

"Just for that, no brownies for you."

Evie laughed.

COLIN HUNG UP THE phone with a sigh as Tom walked in with an armful of files.

"Everything okay?"

"Yeah, it's fine."

Tom set the files down on the desk.

"I thought Deputy Asher wanted to speak with me?"

"I'm sure you couldn't avoid her if you tried."

"I didn't see anything, I promise. I told Sheriff Arnetto everything the night Deirdre was killed." The young man looked anxious.

"I know you did, Tom. Everything's going to be okay, I promise."

God, I hope everything's going to be okay, he prayed fervently.

Colin felt stretched thin, the events of the last few days wearing him down. Yesterday he'd had to tackle the guest room, which was covered in Deirdre's blood – he was going to have to repaint, among other things – and the grief that had overwhelmed him as he stared at the bloodstains on the carpet was deep and frustrating. He could only imagine how Tom must feel, having found Deirdre in the first place.

"Tom, why don't you take a few days off? I'm sure Candace and I can handle things here."

But Tom shook his head, adamant.

"I appreciate the thought, Colin, but it's better to have work. Besides, the Harvest Festival is barely a week away, and there's already too much for three people to handle."

"It might not be safe to hang around, Tom."

"Fuck it," scowled Tom, "If some bastard wants to come after you, they're going to have to go through me first."

Colin grinned to cover the swell of emotion.

"Well, in that case, get back to work."

Tom saluted.

"Yes, sir."

EVIE STARED AT THE corkboard covered in photographs and scribbled notes and sighed. At this point, half the town could be the killer. She'd managed to knock a few names off the list, but there was too much ground to cover – too many suspects, too many loose ends.

Tony came up next to her and leaned against her desk in the main room of the Sheriff's Department. Late afternoon sun streamed through the windows as Tony handed her a cup of coffee.

"You sound the way I feel."

"Thanks. I keep thinking if I stare at it long enough, the killer's just going to pop up and be totally obvious."

"Unfortunately, it doesn't work that way. And I hate to do it, but I have to add one more problem to our growing pile of shit."

"What's that?" Evie sipped her coffee, strong and black, the way she liked it.

"Over the next week, we're going to have thousands of people coming in for the Harvest Festival. Not only is it going to be harder to pick out any suspicious behavior, but we're going to be stretched thin regardless – there's no way we can keep up security."

"So what do we do?"

Tony started moving photographs from one end of the corkboard to the other – Candace, Tom, Colin.

"Let's focus security on Colin and his staff. The killer is going to strike close to home, and Candace and Tom are like family. So we'll focus on this column."

"So I've been informed," Evie muttered, sour.

Tony grabbed a notepad from the desk and scrawled on it, and then ripped the sheet off and tacked it up under Tom's picture.

Evie Asher.

"Hey!" Evie protested.

"Evie, your love life is none of my business, but I'd have to be blind to miss the fact that you've got our young mayor wrapped around your prickly little finger."

"Hardly," she scoffed.

Tony folded his arms and held her gaze, steady.

"Protest all you like, but the killer's already seen the two of you together, and I have absolute proof that you are high on his or her target list."

"I'm sorry," she whispered.

"Don't be sorry," insisted Tony, "You're allowed to have a life, and personally I think it would be great for Colin to wind up with someone who's as much of a control freak as he is. But your timing sucks."

"What do we do next?"

"Well, we've got a call in to the pharmacy to confirm Candace's alibi, we've basically eliminated all of Colin's paramours and business associates. I'm at a loss. What do you think?"

Evie examined the board for a moment and then moved two photos to the center, and then stood back.

"Dreyer Morton or Millicent Grayson?" Tony sounded surprised.

"Millicent has been impossible to track down – every time I try to get hold of her to ask a few questions, she's unavailable. The scuttlebutt is that she has a thing for Colin, and seems a little possessive about him."

"Poor girl. Her husband was lost at sea. They never even found the body." Tony revealed.

"That might be enough to drive a person over the edge – alone with a young son to raise, fixated on a kind, successful man who has the gall to ignore her advances."

Tony nodded, reflective.

"Well, check it out, though I don't know. It seems like a stretch – she doesn't look like she could harm a fly. What about Dreyer Morton?"

"It's no secret that he hates Colin for having a relationship with his daughter."

Tony snorted, dismissive.

"If it wasn't Althea, Dreyer would find eight reasons to hate Colin before breakfast. The man was furious that Hank Daniels was elected mayor instead of him, and figured when he died that he'd finally get his chance. Then the Council backed Colin and that was that. He was pretty pissed – he's on the Council himself."

"They didn't even consider him?"

"You catch more flies with honey, Asher, and Dreyer is nine-tenths vinegar. Besides, he already owns half the town. I'm guessing folks figured that a man can have too much power."

Evie stretched carefully.

"How are you feeling?"

"I'm good."

Tony scrutinized her carefully.

"Go home. Case or no case, you're still healing. I'll have a couple of guys meet you up there."

Evie was about to protest, but knew he was right, and a nap and a bath sounded good. Instead, she nodded.

"Think you can convince Dreyer Morton to come down here for a chat?"

"Without a fully prepped legal team? Maybe. I'll give it a shot." Tony grinned and pointed to the door. "Out. That's an order."

THE ASHER CABIN WAS silent, as it had been before Fran Asher's granddaughter had moved back to town, and brought her life of sin and corruption with her. Like father, like daughter. Her mother at least had realized that the world was better off without her kind and had taken care of the problem. If only Laura's bullet had killed her husband instead of just wounding him, but no, his corruption had seeped into young Evie Asher, and now she was back, luring Colin in with her soft curves.

SLUT COP. It won't stand.

Killing Deirdre had been satisfying, especially after the rage that overflowed at the sight of Colin pleasuring the Asher woman out on the porch, for God and the entire world to see. He'd used his hands and mouth, and even from the secluded spot in the woods, the pleasure and satisfaction on the woman's face was evident. And intolerable. The shots were meant to hurt, to rid the world of another succubus, but the fear of hitting Colin was too great, so accuracy was impossible. He needed to live, in order to be corrected.

And then we can be together.

The sound of approaching cars meant visitors, and there was work to be done. Hasty now, red spray paint staining the latex gloves as the message was laid out.

This was the last warning, but really, it was meaningless, because no matter what –

Evie Asher had to die.

CHAPTER ELEVEN

EVIE WAS NUMB AS she made the short drive from her house to Colin's. The giant red SLUT spray painted across the front of Gram's beloved cabin was a violation, a reminder that she was in the killer's sights. The feeling of helplessness and fury had fused together into an icy rage that left her surprisingly calm, and then numb as she gave her statement to Tony. Together with Zeke and a couple of volunteers, they had scoured the area – more wasted hours.

Inside the cabin, Evie had been shocked to find evidence of tampering – nothing was missing, but objects had been moved. Her skin crawled at the thought of the killer touching her things, invading her space. By the time she and Tony had finished dusting for prints and taking pictures, it was dark.

She had protested when Tony ordered her over to Colin's place for the night – the place was under heavy guard already, and there was no way Evie was spending the night at her cabin tonight.

"It's just going to provoke the bastard," she insisted.

"I think at this point you could be halfway around the world and still be in danger. At least if you're both in one place I can keep an eye on you."

Too upset and exhausted to argue, Evie had simply climbed into her car and headed over. As she pulled up in the driveway, she took note of an unfamiliar silver minivan.

Evie forced a nonchalant smile for the guards as she walked up to the porch and knocked. A moment later, the door was wrenched open, and Colin looked down at her, his eyes filled with surprise and relief.

"Deputy Asher! Come in, please."

Bemused, she let him take her backpack and usher her into the living room, where Millicent Grayson sat, nursing a cup of coffee. She was wearing a tight, low-cut red sweater and a short skirt, and looked more than a little annoyed to see Evie. Realization slammed into Evie – she'd interrupted an attempted seduction. But unlike the last time, when it was clear that Colin was enthusiastically encouraging Deirdre's advances with a few of his own, now he seemed almost desperate to get away.

Serves you right, thought Evie, as Colin propelled her forward.

"Millie, have you met Evie?"

Reluctantly, Millicent shook hands.

"Nice to meet you, Deputy. Your grandmother was a wonderful woman. She's missed in this community."

"Thanks. I've been trying to get a hold of you, Miss Grayson. I have a few questions, if you don't mind."

"Actually, this isn't the best time – " began Millicent, angling herself a little toward Colin.

"It's a perfect time," Colin assured Evie, putting her between them.

Evie was amused, but swallowed the smile that threatened.

"Can you tell me where you were Monday night, Millicent?"

"I was home. My son Lloyd was sick."

"Did anyone see you?"

"No, I was home alone."

"Did you make any calls?"

"No." Millicent turned to Colin, her eyes wide and scared, "Colin, what is this?"

"Just routine questions," Evie insisted, soothingly, "We're questioning anyone who might have a connection to Colin. Everyone he works with, everyone he's dated, and so on."

Millicent blushed.

"Colin has been wonderful since my husband died. But he and I are just friends," she murmured. *So far.* The words were unspoken, but hung in the air between them. Behind her, Evie could hear Colin mutter, "Shit," under his breath.

"Millie, maybe we should have coffee another day. Deputy Asher and I have some police business to go over."

Millicent frowned, but set her cup down.

"Are you sure? I don't want you staying here alone."

Some demon prompted Evie to speak up. "There's security guarding the house until the threat has passed, and I'll be staying here tonight as well."

She turned to look at Colin and caught the flare of heat in his eyes, but he tamped down on it before smiling gently at Millicent.

"See? Safe and sound. I promise."

Millicent bit her lip, but gathered her coat, stopping to give Colin a hug, which he returned.

"If you need *anything*, I'm just a phone call away."

"I'll see you out."

With a barely civil nod at Evie, Millicent let Colin lead her out of the living room.

Evie used the moment alone to gather herself, and a sense of inevitability settled over her. She knew what she was about to do was a monumentally terrible idea, but she didn't want to fight it anymore. It rankled that some deranged stalker had labeled her a slut, and was punishing her for leading Colin Daniels down a dark, sexual path. It rankled even more that aside from some mind-blowing heavy petting, she was innocent of the accusations.

If I'm going to be branded a nymphomaniac, the least I deserve is a couple of screaming orgasms to validate it, she reasoned, all of her past reluctance and worries swamped by the thought of finally getting what she'd wanted since the moment she stepped foot in Bright's Ferry.

Colin returned to the room, leaning thoughtfully against the doorway.

"You don't really think she killed Deirdre, do you?"

"I can't rule it out." Evie hoped her hands weren't shaking as she tried to figure out the best way to broach the subject she really wanted to talk about.

"Do you really mean that, or are you just jealous?" he teased.

Evie blustered. *Of course I'm jealous. That doesn't mean I have to admit it.*

Rather than answer, she stalked past him and headed upstairs, her pulse pounding. Behind her, she felt Colin hesitate, and then follow. Outside his bedroom door, she stopped and turned to face him.

"Is there anyone in this town who doesn't want to fuck you?" The words came out harsher than Evie had intended.

"What are you doing here, Evie?" His voice was soft, heated, and she couldn't meet his gaze.

She reached for the buttons of his shirt instead. A rough yank and they gave way, pinging across the floor.

COLIN LOST HIS BREATH as Evie ripped his shirt open to flatten her hands against his chest. The skin-to-skin contact was so unexpected, so delicious, that he shuddered, hardening so swiftly that it was almost painful.

Evie's lower lip was trembling, and her eyes were lowered, focused on the flesh she explored with greedy, but oddly tentative strokes. He realized with a shock that she was scared as Hell. Scared of what? That he'd reject her? *Fat fucking chance.*

The spark between them was off the charts, but the memory that made him quake was Evie on the porch, bare and glowing with sexual satisfaction, the taste of her sweet pussy lingering on his tongue as she shyly invited him inside. The first hint of trust.

Trust that had been trampled as Evie spent the week interviewing the women he'd slept with. As a result, she probably expected something meaningless and fast, a sweaty drive to climax that would leave them physically satiated, but not require any more commitment than a couple of hours of her gorgeous body straining against his. A quick fuck that would leave her wounded heart out of it, and let her get on with her life, her defenses intact.

Colin was stunned to find that he didn't want that. Not with Evie. She'd come to him and they were going to do this right. He wanted it to mean something to her. What exactly, he wasn't sure, but Colin wanted her to remember him, to wipe all memory of other lovers out of her head until she was as obsessed with him as he was coming to be with her. If that made her uncomfortable, he'd just have to make her come again and again, until she was too unglued to think about it.

He licked his suddenly dry lips, thinking about how responsive she was as Evie scraped his nipples with sharp little fingernails and stroked a path downward. His cock jerked.

"You came over to sleep with me." His voice was harsh, hands still clenched at his sides.

"Are you going to turn me down?" she asked as though that were an actual possibility.

"Not on your life. But we're going to do this my way." Of that, Colin was sure.

Evie frowned.

"That's not what – "

No more arguments.

"Shut up and strip."

THE DEMAND SENT A wave of heat through Evie's veins, but she ignored Colin, reaching for his belt, surprised to find her hands were shaking as she tried to work the buckle. She couldn't believe she'd ripped his shirt. His chest was as gorgeous as she remembered, miles of hard muscle, warm and alive and begging to be touched. *Fucking buckle.* She jerked at it.

"Shit."

"Evie."

Colin's hands closed over hers and she looked up, startled, and caught her breath at the hunger in his eyes. Holding her gaze, he helped her slowly open his belt, undo the single button, and carefully slide the zipper down over the heavy bulge beneath. The eroticism of the simple act had her pussy throbbing, already damp with need.

Evie freed her fingers from his and looked down.

Colin sucked in a breath as she traced the soft arrow of hair under his navel, and then slid past the waistband of his boxer briefs to wrap her fingers around his cock, hot and huge, the size of him making her own breath catch in her throat.

"God, baby," he groaned, his head falling back as she learned him, stroking and squeezing, and using her other hand to shove his clothing down his body, wanting him completely bare to her. He shrugged off the remains of his shirt.

Fully naked, he was a beautiful animal – warm skin poured over muscle, big and hot and tight, the proof of his arousal thick and long and deliciously hard for her. The shaft rose proudly from a neat thatch of dark hair over a heavy sac, the wide head rosy and glistening, promising pleasure and more pleasure and more pleasure. No wonder women threw themselves at him all the time – he should be carved out of marble, gracing a museum pedestal somewhere.

Evie frowned at the thought of his other conquests. Noting that her fingers had stilled, Colin pried his eyes open. His hazel eyes were predatory and very, very hot.

"Problem?"

Casual and meaningless, Asher. Who cares if he's got the sex life of a horny tomcat? Just get him out of your system. That sounded kind of rational, Evie thought. She squeezed the throbbing flesh in her palm again and he groaned, thrusting up into her hand, filling her with satisfaction at his helpless reaction to her touch. *All mine.*

Okay, less rational.

"Didn't I tell you to strip?" Colin's voice was soft, but unmistakably commanding.

Evie waited for her hackles to rise as they did when Jack bossed her around in the bedroom. She'd preferred him courteous and charming, and his attempts to dominate always left her feeling uncomfortable. With Colin, all she felt was a humiliatingly intense rush of heat to her throbbing clit that left her confused and wary.

But she had no time to examine the feelings, because he wasted no time, stripping off her shirt himself and twisting the front clasp of her bra, peeling back the cups. The righteous indignation she was trying to work up melted as he shaped her breasts with talented hands, rolling the nipples to hard, aching peaks.

"Fucking sweet," he murmured, and captured one nipple with his mouth to drive her mad with hot, wet suction and gentle scrapes of his teeth.

Her knees buckled at the sensation and the harsh, sexual tone, and the next thing she knew, Colin was moving them into the bedroom, leaving their pile of clothes on the hallway floor. Inside, he kicked the door closed and wrenched the quilt back from the bed before lowering her to the mattress. He reached over to turn on the bedside lamp and the room was flooded with soft light. Propping himself over her, Colin returned his attention to her breasts, his cock a rigid length against her thigh.

"I love your nipples," he rasped, flicking one with his tongue, "So plump and eager to be sucked. The prettiest dusky pink. Is that tasty little clit the same color? I'll bet it's swollen and hot for me."

He made quick work of the button of her jeans, and Evie jerked as two long fingers slipped under her panties, wickedly circled her clit, and then eased inside in a mind-numbing slide. Evie writhed under him, trying to increase the pace as he slowly thrust his fingers deeper, but he held her pinned with his big body, worshipping her breasts with his mouth.

God, that feels good.

Colin let her nipple go with a last little nip and moved to the other one. She strained against him, feeling the tension coil low in her abdomen.

"Please, Colin – "

"You're drenching my fingers, baby. Hot, tight little pussy, you're going to wrap around my cock like a glove. I can feel you pulsing. Does that mean you're ready to come?"

She wouldn't answer – a girl could only give up so much.

"Nothing to say?"

Colin twisted his fingers in a move that sent lightning streaking along every nerve ending, and his thumb came up to flick her throbbing clit once, twice, again. She cried out.

"Let go, Evie," he urged, and bit down gently on her nipple as his thumb circled and pressed, and his fingers plunged deep.

Evie detonated into a million pieces, stars sparking behind her eyelids as pleasure rained down on her body. She was barely aware that she was arching up, straining to feed as much of her breast into his mouth as he could take while his fingers masterfully stroked and flicked her to another dizzying peak. Evie winced internally as he finally let her come down, pretty sure she'd shouted his name that last time.

He chuckled, and she would have smacked him, but her whole body was tingling in delight, eager for more. She'd smack him later.

"If that's how you come when you're determined to be difficult, Evie, I can't wait to see you cooperate."

Colin pulled his fingers free as she glared at him, but a blush raced up her cheeks when he sucked the glistening digits into mouth for a leisurely taste. Still smirking, he pulled off her jeans, boots, and panties, and finally they were naked together on the bed.

Evie felt her heart quake as Colin sat back on his heels, his eyes hot and hungry as they perused her from head to toe. His fingers traced the edge of the bandage on her side. She had the crazy urge to cover herself, but if this was going to be the one night she permitted herself with Colin Daniels, she was going to shove her inhibitions aside and take everything he had to offer. So instead, she cupped her breasts, pinching her nipples lightly, and watched his pupils dilate.

"Look at you," he whispered, "Watching you play with those pretty tits, I could come just like this."

He wrapped a hand around his shaft, unabashedly stroking himself as he followed her movements, rapt. A bead of fluid glimmered on the fat crown, and Evie's mouth watered for a taste.

"Don't you dare," she ordered, and in one swift move she was up and leaning over his cock to lap the bead from the sensitive tip, bracing one hand against his hip as she tasted him.

Mmm…salt and musk and Colin.

She licked again and heard his moan above her. His thighs were rigid as he slid a hand into her hair to cup the back of her head, holding her to him.

"Keep that up and I'm going to spend the night fucking your sweet mouth, baby." He permitted himself one luxurious thrust that filled her with several throbbing inches.

"Okay," she murmured agreeably as she pulled back, brushing his hand aside to track a vein down the thick length of his shaft with her tongue. The taste of him was heady, addictive, and her pussy pulsed when she drew the wide head back between her lips for a decadent suckle.

"Later," he groaned, and Evie made a soft noise of disapproval as he pulled away.

Colin urged her to her back as he reached into the night stand for a condom, rolling it on swiftly before coming down over her, face to face, her breasts crushed against his chest, her hips cradling his, and the thick heat of his cock pressing into her soft pussy.

He kissed her, his tongue sliding into her mouth, and she whimpered against him as the full-body sensation threatened to overwhelm her. Pausing, Colin searched her features, his hazel eyes intense, and suddenly Evie couldn't take it.

Too intimate.

Too scary.

He saw too much and that terrified her. She turned her face away.

"Evie – "

"Just fuck me," she whispered.

"We're going to talk about this." His voice was deep and soft, but brooked no argument.

"No we're not."

Not until Hell freezes over, she thought.

Suddenly Colin pulled back, but before Evie could feel rejected, he had flipped her over and yanked her to her knees. With a gentle hand between her shoulder blades, Colin pressed her breasts to the bed. The position left her ass in the air, on display. Evie felt exposed and uncomfortably aroused as he spread her thighs wide and just *looked* for a long moment. She knew she was wet and swollen, and the heat filling her body had her fingers clenching in the sheets.

"Colin – "

"Hold still." He punctuated the order with a light slap to one ass cheek, and all thoughts of protesting the unfamiliar position vanished as fire raced to her clit. Evie was appalled – she'd enjoyed that far more than she should.

Colin gently traced the bare folds of her pussy, and Evie felt shock race through her as one slick finger slid between her cheeks to tease the rosette of her anus. Before she could decide whether she liked the startling stroke of sensation, it was replaced by the blunt head of his cock, pressing against her in a hot, persuasive kiss.

"One day, I'm going to take you here, Evie. But for now – "

They both groaned as he slid the crown down through her slick folds and snuggled it against her opening. Evie had never felt more helpless, spread and waiting to be filled, wet and panting and – *Oh God, just do it already!*

She was vaguely horrified with herself. Despite the protests of her feminist core – *I am not submissive or docile,* she assured herself – Evie was startled find that once again she liked Colin taking control of her body, pleasuring her any way he wanted to. Still, it rankled.

"You know, it's not fair," she admitted, breathless, "You make me feel completely out of control." Evie pushed back, biting her lip at the feel of the head parting her folds. But instead of filling her up, *the bastard*, Colin held her hips steady.

"You think you're the only one who feels that way?" he countered, "You turn me into a caveman. All I want to do is drag you back to my lair and keep you naked and open so that I can do *this* until we're both too tired to move."

This was his cock pressing into her tight sheath. Evie cried out as the thick flesh rasped across sensitive nerve endings, and her delicate muscles yielded to too many inches of hot, heavy shaft.

"Fuck, you're tight. You okay?"

Her fingers curled into the sheets. She licked her lips, panting.

"You're...big."

"Just a little more." He rocked his hips, nudging even deeper.

More?!

It was too much, but that didn't prevent her from arching her back, tilting her hips for the last inch that pressed her ass against him, the sensation of being impaled to the hilt overwhelming and incredible, his heavy sac cushioned against the damp pad of her pussy.

"Hard and fast," she demanded.

"Uh-uh," murmured Colin, "My turn to be in charge."

He gripped her hips and started moving, and Evie lost her train of thought. It was hard to stay annoyed when the man was treating her pussy to such a slow, delicious fuck, each stroke bringing her closer, driving her higher. This was *beyond* good.

Colin leaned over her, changing the angle, twining his fingers with hers, and though she couldn't see his face, she could feel his breath, his heartbeat pulsing deep within her, and his hard muscled body hot against hers. *Too intimate*, her heart warned, but the slow, deep thrusts were driving her crazy, and she couldn't focus on the emotional alarm bell right at this particular moment in time.

"More," she begged, and couldn't even feel bad about it.

"As much as you want, baby," he agreed, sounding a little smug, but he fucked her harder, so she decided to forgive him.

Colin slid one hand under her to caress her stomach, and then moved down between her thighs to trace the taut edge where he stretched her with a feather light touch that had her gasping.

"Greedy little pussy," he murmured, breathless, "You're taking all of me so sweetly."

Not altering his rhythm, Colin's fingers found her clit, flicking it slowly in the way he'd learned she liked. She cried out and he nuzzled the side of her face, nibbling on her jaw.

"Come for me one more time," he ordered.

And for one of the few times in their rocky association, Evie did exactly as she was told.

CHAPTER TWELVE

COLIN BARELY HAD THE presence of mind to pull away from Evie's soft flesh and deal with the condom before he fell back against the pillows and tugged her to his chest. Pleasure still zinged through him from the most intense orgasm he'd ever experienced, doubled by the way she came around him, milking his cock with the most exquisite pressure, her throaty cries like music.

Colin tried to drum up some remorse for having mounted Evie Asher and fucked her like an animal but all he felt was a sense of bone-deep satisfaction as she cuddled against him, her tongue reaching out to lap softly at his nipple while a soft sound of contentment escaped her throat. The nipple beaded under her tongue, and he felt an answering twitch in the vicinity of his cock, but surely that wasn't possible because she'd wrung him dry.

"That was…good," she murmured, and he felt like a fucking hero.

Evie scraped fingernails along his abs and his dick took definite notice.

Then she sighed.

Colin knew that the first words out of her mouth would be serious, pulling them out of this hazy sexual cocoon and back to harsh reality.

Not yet.

He rolled her, pinning her to the bed, taking her lips in a hard and mind-stealing kiss, but before she had a chance to protest, he was kissing his way down to those perfect tits and lower. When she realized his intent, she froze, sinking her fingers into his hair. Colin paused at her navel, licking and nuzzling the cute little cup. After a moment or two, he felt her clench her fingers, the nails grazing his scalp as she pushed him down.

Oh yeah, he thought, her unspoken demand a total turn-on. Which was interesting. Colin was used to taking the lead in bed, and his girlfriends generally preferred it. The image of submitting to Evie, letting her pleasure him and fuck him any way she wanted to, sent an uncomfortably intense surge of arousal through him, and he shuddered.

We'll have to try that. Next time.

Colin used his shoulders to spread Evie's thighs wide, and then cupped her ass, lifting her to him. She was soft and wet and swollen, and his mouth watered for her. He felt her startled intake of breath as he feasted, coaxing her arousal higher and higher, feeling her shake in release as he suckled her sweet clit. Then he started all over again, until she was twisting against his mouth, attempting to get closer, fingers clutching his hair, trying to pull him where she needed him to be. The erotic little tugs had his cock up to full salute in no time at all.

"Oh God…Colin…please – "

When she was panting, *begging* for him, he surged up, half-frantic himself, donned another condom with lightning speed, and turned her to the side so that her hips were perched on the edge of the mattress, and then stood, pushing her thighs apart to make space for himself. He positioned his throbbing dick at her core.

"Hard and fast?" he asked, his voice a rough growl of arousal.

Eyes gleaming and unfocused, Evie nodded, her hands reaching up to twisting in the sheets over her head, pushing her breasts up.

Unceremoniously, Colin wrapped her legs around his hips and plunged deep into liquid heat, noting with satisfaction how those perfect tits jiggled deliciously with each stroke. He pounded into her until her eyes went dark and she screamed out her release. With a shout, he followed her over, letting the waves of pleasure wash over him before he collapsed, barely managing to catch himself on one arm to avoid crushing her.

In a tangle of limbs, he hauled her up the bed and leaned over to kill the light and dispose of condom number two. At this rate, neither of them would be able to walk by the end of the night.

Colin wrapped his arms around her, cuddling his cheek against her breasts, and was supremely gratified when her hands came up to hold him close.

"We have to talk," she murmured, but the ominous statement was broken by a yawn.

"We will," he responded, half-asleep. "Tomorrow."

They were both asleep in seconds.

SUNLIGHT STREAMED THROUGH THE windows as Evie stretched, which only pressed her body more tightly against Colin Daniels, who tucked her closer but didn't wake, the stubble on his jaw rasping against her nipple in an unconscious move that sent tingles running through her, though she was barely awake.

Evie couldn't remember the last time she had slept so well.

But phenomenal sex will do that, she thought wryly as awareness returned.

Colin was wrapped around her like a living blanket, one leg thrown over hers and a sizable morning erection prodding her thigh. It was the thought of what she wanted to do with that thick flesh, *what she had already done*, that had a wave of panic welling up. Suddenly desperate for a little space, she eased out from under him , shoving a pillow into his arms to cuddle. She stood naked by the bed, staring down at the rumpled, sleeping sex god who had taken control and pleasured her like no other, and a wave of hot and cold rushed over her. She shivered.

Okay, Asher. You've fucked him out of your system, now go take a shower and get on with your life.

That sounded sensible enough, but as Evie hurried into the bathroom, she was newly startled by her image in the mirror. Her lips and nipples were still swollen from his mouth, and reddened scrapes on her thighs and torso showed where his stubble had rubbed her sensitive flesh. A bluish bruise under her right nipple had her yelping in shock – he'd given her a hickey. She looked comprehensively debauched – tasted and marked and well-fucked, her intimate muscles sore from his thorough possession.

"Oh God," she muttered, and jumped into the shower, scrubbing hard to erase all traces of the night before. It wasn't guilt she was feeling about giving in to her desire for the hot young mayor. *That* she had gone into with her eyes open, full steam ahead. It was shame that she was desperate to do it again, to let him have her every night for as long as this insane chemistry burned between them.

But that would mean they were having an affair. And it wouldn't be long before everybody knew about it and started poking into the corners of her life. And then it would blow up in her face, as the residents of Bright's Ferry realized that their precious Mr. Daniels had shacked up with a homewrecker.

Evie groaned as she shut off the water. It was too much to stress over before her first cup of coffee, and besides, she was pretty sure Colin was going to throw a fit when he found out about the latest incident. She still had a killer to catch.

Sighing, Evie reached for a towel.

"YOU SPEND A LOT of time in my house all wet," Colin rumbled, propping himself up against the pillows to admire the delectable sight of Evie coming out of the bathroom in nothing but a towel, "Although the naked is a pleasant development."

A drop of water rolled from her throat down between her breasts, and he was suddenly very thirsty.

"Good morning," she managed, and he could see that her nerves were back.

"Drop the towel," he ordered, and watched a shiver run through her.

Of course she ignored him and opened the bedroom door to grab her shirt and bra from the hallway floor.

"I have to get going."

"You're not inspiring me with much morning-after confidence," he teased and she rolled her eyes, shaking out her shirt.

Colin knew his eyes were predatory, but he couldn't help it as Evie stepped toward the bed to grab her discarded jeans, and every muscle tensed. Waiting for just the right moment, he pounced, and managed to grab a handful of towel. Evie screeched as it came away from her body. Colin couldn't even feel ashamed of the juvenile move because there she was, naked and damp and absolutely breathtaking.

"There, you got a good look. Happy now?" Evie glared at him, temper sparking, and threw her arms out in disgust.

"I'd be happier if you brought that luscious little body over here and let me give it a proper good morning."

Colin pushed the sheet away from his hips to give her a good look at his straining cock. Her eyes widened and she swallowed, licking her lips as if she were remembering the thick flesh filling her mouth. He certainly was.

"I can't," she whispered, frozen. She had apparently forgotten that she was still naked.

"Can't or won't?"

The question was not destined to be answered because at that moment the phone rang. Scowling, Colin picked it up, half-distracted by Evie hastily turning around to pull her panties on, treating him to a glimpse of the perfect curve of her ass.

"Yeah, Tony, what's up? Hang on, let me check and see if she's up."

He pressed the phone to his chest and quirked an eyebrow.

"See? I'm protecting your virtue, Miss Asher. Doesn't that deserve a reward?"

Expertly twisting into her bra, she stomped up to the bed and reached for the phone, and Colin took advantage of the move to yank her down to his chest and capture her mouth in a scorching kiss, pleased as punch at the nails that dug into his ribs and the little whimper that left her throat as he let her go.

"You are such a prick," she whispered, breathless.

Colin grinned and handed her the phone, holding her captive.

"Hey, Tony. No, you didn't wake me. Yes, uh huh. That's great, we can find out if he has an alibi for last night. Okay, see you there in an hour."

Colin was distracted, sucking on the curve of her neck as Evie hung up the phone. She permitted the caress for a moment, and his dick throbbed hopefully against the softness of her stomach, and then she pushed him away. Colin settled back into the pillows with a regretful sigh. Her armor was definitely back up. He wasn't surprised that the fact irked him, but the feeling of hurt was uncomfortably sharp.

"What's up?"

"Dreyer Morton has graciously decided to grant us an interview to discuss his whereabouts the night of the murder and the fact that he totally hates your guts."

"He's all hot air, Evie."

"Still, he's on my list. And I want to grill him about yesterday."

Colin saw her wince and realized that she hadn't meant to say anything.

"What happened yesterday?" His voice dropped a register, suspicious.

"Nothing important." She shrugged into her shirt and hastily pulled on her jeans. "Got any coffee around here? I'm going to go see if the guys outside want any before they change shift."

She was barely done babbling before she was out the door.

Frowning, Colin reached for the phone.

EVIE HEARD HIM POUNDING down the stairs before she saw him, and leaned over the percolating coffee pot, closing her eyes in a silent prayer, which she knew was probably a wasted effort at this point.

"What the fuck, Evie!"

Yep, furious.

She looked up and tried not to drool. Practically vibrating with anger, Colin had stormed into the sunny kitchen in nothing but a pair of low-slung jeans he hadn't bothered to fasten.

"Well?"

She was supposed to answer him?

Evie tried to focus, but her thoughts were arrested by the insidious idea that if he really were her boyfriend, she would be perfectly within her rights to explore all that hard muscle, and he'd go willingly when she pressed him back to the scrubbed butcher block table. He'd just have to take it as she climbed up and petted his hard body all over, his big cock straining against the zipper of those

136

open jeans. Her pussy clenched at the thought of peeling back the denim to free his shaft, and then picking up where she left off last night, when her oral exploration of that thick stalk was interrupted by his not unreasonable need to fuck her silly. This time, she'd taste every inch at her leisure, and he'd just have to surrender…

"Keep looking at me like that and I'm going to take you on the counter, Evie." His voice was gravely and hot, but still angry, "After you explain why you didn't bother to tell me that your house was *vandalized* yesterday afternoon."

"I was going to tell you," she sighed, but the words sounded petulant, even to her.

"The other night was a warning. That's why the stalker didn't kill us. And now he's after you."

"Good," said Evie, grimly.

"Good? Are you out of your mind?"

"I apparently piss this lunatic off enough to vandalize my house in broad daylight. Anger leads to stupidity."

Colin stepped forward to grab her shoulders.

"You are *not* going to use yourself as bait. I won't allow it."

Evie shrugged out of his grip, irritated.

"You don't tell me what to do! I am the law enforcement officer, you are the pretty boy Mayor with the stalker problem."

"And you don't have any idea who that stalker is!"

Evie poked him in the chest.

"For your information, I've narrowed it down to a short list."

"Who?"

Evie started to answer, and then stopped. She'd already shared too much with him, both in terms of the investigation and her life. Every suggested suspect was met with disbelief from Colin, who trusted his friends and his community too much to really believe that one of them could harbor something so evil and dark. And now they'd slept together, and her growing emotional attachment to him was going to cloud her judgment. It was time to set some hard boundaries she should have set the moment the problem began. Before one of them got seriously hurt.

Ready to start paying attention, Asher? Her inner cop sniffed in contempt.

"I can't talk about an ongoing investigation," Evie blurted out, and watched the thunderclouds gather on Colin's face.

"You can't be serious."

"From now on, all information is on a need-to-know basis. I'm already going to go down as the worst cop in history for getting involved with the focus of an open case, I'd rather not make matters worse. You will not be present at any interviews, investigations, or crime scenes. You will be briefed only as occasion warrants it by Sheriff Arnetto or myself. You will maintain a security escort at all times, avoid open windows, and stay off the street until I tell you it's safe. In fact, as of right now, I'm putting you on home protection. You step one foot outside that door and you'll be sorry. Do I make myself clear?"

"You can't just – "

"Oh yes, I can."

Ignoring his blustering attempt to regroup and come up with a suitably scathing response to her set of orders, Evie calmly poured herself a cup of coffee and walked out.

Chapter Thirteen

EVIE KNEW THAT DREYER Morton could be a haughty, self-righteous son-of-a-bitch, but she hadn't realized that he could be a shrewd, calculating businessman with a spine of steel. Which made sense, given that he owned half the town and showed no desire to retire and hand the reins of his empire over to the next generation.

She, Tony, and Dreyer sat at a table together in the small conference room at the Sheriff's Department. They had no interrogation room, but really, until recently the department hadn't needed one. The simple wooden table and beige-slatted blinds seemed a little too ordinary for the discussion of murder that Evie was about to dive into.

"My great-great-grandfather came to Bright's Ferry after the Civil War," remarked Dreyer, "He was the first freed black slave to set foot in this community, and he took one look at the bay and knew he'd come home."

"I'm not accusing you of anything," Evie began.

"Yes, young lady, you are. By calling me in here and questioning my whereabouts on the night of Miss Small's unfortunate murder, you're suggesting that I had something to do with it, or at the very least that I am withholding information that would allow you to sniff out the killer."

He leaned forward, gripping his cane.

"And what I am telling you is that my family has roots in this town that go back a hundred and fifty years. To insinuate that I would allow a murderer to desecrate my family's land is an insult."

"Easy, Dreyer," muttered Tony, "The town's littered with people who have been here forever. I can name ten families that were here a hundred years before yours."

Dreyer glared at him, and Evie started again.

"It's obvious that you and Colin don't have the most...agreeable...relationship."

"I think my feelings about our mayor have been made quite clear. But that doesn't mean that I would stoop to physically harming him, or any woman unfortunate enough to be seduced."

Evie forced herself to not squirm in her seat as Dreyer continued.

"Of course, my Althea had nothing to do with it, but surely there has to be someone on his long list of conquests that holds a grudge."

Evie bit her lip, but held her temper.

"We are investigating all of our options, Mr. Morton, and the fact remains that you have no alibi for the incidents in question."

"Miss Asher, do I look like a man who would take potshots at your house from the woods?"

"Alibi," Evie insisted.

Dreyer sighed, disgusted.

"It highly insulting to be harassed in this fashion, but for your information, I spend most of my time home alone. If you insist on pursuing this nonsensical course of action, feel free to review my video security system. It will show you that I was precisely where I said I would be."

Evie exchanged a wary glance with Tony, who shrugged.

"Thanks for coming in, Dreyer. I'll send Zeke over to pick up those tapes."

Dreyer hesitated.

"I'd prefer you review them yourself, Sheriff. As you know, I work from home and they contain some rather, sensitive business dealings that I would rather not share with the general public."

Tony's eyebrow went up, but he nodded, "Sure. Why don't you let me know when might be a good time to stop by and we'll take care of it."

Dreyer looked relieved, and even managed to be gracious about shaking Evie's hand. On the way out the door, he paused.

"Miss Asher, the other day at the funeral – I may have overstepped my bounds. Slightly. You are not to blame for the unfortunate transgressions of your parents, which no doubt led to your own reckless mistakes. That being said, your grandmother would have me skinned alive for speaking to you like that. She was a formidable and wonderful woman, and to honor her memory, I apologize."

With that he tipped his hat and swept out of the room, his cane tapping on the floor, leaving Evie flummoxed by the backhanded apology.

"So, I'm still a fallen woman, but it's not my fault because my parents sucked?"

"With Dreyer, that's probably the best you're going to get. Accept it and move on," grinned Tony.

Evie shook her head in disbelief and headed out to uncover the cork board and move Dreyer's name to the general pool.

"We should go over those tapes, but I've changed my mind about Dreyer Morton. He's more likely to just stab Colin in the heart with that cane in Main Square than go to all this trouble. He's not a man who likes to apologize or explain his actions, and I can't see him hiding his feelings toward Colin or going to such lengths to avoid recognition."

"Yeah, he'd rather spend his time trying to get him thrown out of office. So we're down to Millicent Grayson." Tony was skeptical.

"I have to question Tom Castillo, but that seems like a stretch, too."

Evie sighed.

"We can't go on like this. How long are we going to be able to maintain round the clock security for Colin? He can't stay in that house forever. Anything on the red paint?"

"Not purchased in Bright's Ferry, from all accounts, and no prints on anything up at your Gram's cabin. For the moment, you may as well continue to stay at the Daniels place."

Evie felt her cheeks heating.

"That may not be the best idea," she muttered to herself, but nodded.

Spending time with Colin was only going to remind her of what she couldn't allow herself to have. There was too much temptation, and she'd already proven to herself that she had no willpower where he was concerned.

Keep him safe, she ordered herself, *and stay out of his pants.*

THE SLUT COP HAD spent the night. In Colin's bed or not was a mystery – who could get close enough with those thugs guarding the house? Zeke would have been no problem alone – he was a jumpy boy, and always had been. He might grow into a forthright, upstanding deputy someday, but right now he was just a rookie, barely an adult and scared of his own shadow. Slipping by him would be no trouble at all, or knocking him out. A simple blow to the head and he would be down for the count.

The fact remained that the slut cop had spent the night, and though there was no way to tell if she had convinced Colin to sleep with her, to immerse himself in her seductive, poisonous flesh, it was an easy assumption. Evie Asher had been stunned at the damage to her grandmother's precious house, which was delicious, though her expression had been difficult to see from behind the trees. There had only been a moment to enjoy it before Tony's volunteers had arrived, followed by the Sheriff himself – such a sad, lonely man.

And so tragic, what had happened to his wife. But that was a thought for later.

Maybe the paint had been a mistake, born from righteous rage and frustration, but a mistake nonetheless, because now security would be doubled. But they couldn't keep it up forever. Colin would see the error of his ways after Evie was dead.

It was maddening, thinking about Colin and Evie entwined together, her body wrapping around his, choking the life and goodness out of him like a boa constrictor compressing his soul. One had to wonder what he saw in her. She was pretty in an odd sort of way, but her gray eyes were unnerving, and her prickly, unlikable demeanor was far from friendly.

There was nothing to be done about it. Colin needed to be punished, and the Asher woman dealt with. She was getting closer to uncovering the truth. Unfortunately, there were too many guards, too many eyes, and it was increasingly difficult to find a crack in their defenses.

Infuriating.

No, this called for a different sort of punishment. A change of course, a surprise, but a clear understanding that no one was safe, not as long as Colin remained unrepentant, smiling and flirting with women, encouraging their loathsome advances, reveling in sin and lust and heaping disgrace upon his legacy.

A victim was necessary. It couldn't be helped. It was his fault entirely. And if the slut cop was out of reach for the moment, it would have to be someone who deserved it.

Perhaps Grace Mallow. Though she and Colin appeared to be uninterested in each other, he regarded her as a sister, and she was clearly a bad influence. It was obvious from her hair, her clothes, her taste in unwholesome literature and music, and more than anything else, the way she watched Matt Harris with hungry, lustful eyes, sure that no one noticed.

Someone had noticed.

Grace was a good option, and her death would make Colin sit up and pay attention, and protect the young children who visited the library from her corruptive influence.

Imagining it brought a wave of visceral delight that came to an abrupt halt.

Grace was an obvious choice. They would expect that.

Another victim, then. Someone that no one would expect. A tragic loss to the community, and a reminder to Evie Asher no one was safe.

That she was next.

COLIN WAS GOING STIR crazy. Though Tom had stopped by with a crate full of work to keep him busy, he felt like the walls were closing in. Worst of all was the feeling that while he was in here, cocooned like a porcelain doll wrapped in cotton batting, Evie was out there trying to track down a killer. He wanted her safe. He wanted her to let him protect her.

Protect the woman with the gun and the iron-plated armor, he snorted, but frowned as he swiftly remembered that she *had* been hurt. Despite her untouchable supercop façade, she could bleed, and she could die.

No.

Colin paced the living room, even more worked up than before. He was alarmed at how quickly his feelings for Evie were moving beyond just a rabid need to have her under him, and morphing into something deeper, something much scarier. Not that he didn't want her under him again – yes, that was a given – but he wanted to propel her past the fear of intimacy that *Jack, the bastard,* had left her with, and take gentle possession of her fragile heart. It was lunacy, but he was quickly coming to realize that anything less wouldn't do.

But how to convince her?

He sat down on the couch, absently scribbling on a notebook, somewhat sheepish as he looked down long moments later to realize he'd been doodling her name like a smitten teenager. Suddenly, he froze, arrested by the sight of her name in quirky letters on the page.

"The handwriting," he breathed, and jumped up, heading for the front door, "Zeke! Get in here!"

ALAN WILKINSON PUSHED BACK his plate with a contented sigh.

"Wonderful as always, Candy," he said, blowing a kiss to his wife.

Candace smiled.

"Want some more? There's tons."

"You're going to have to roll me to bed, honey. Your chicken and dumplings is the best in the state."

She waved a dismissive hand, but he could see she was pleased with the compliment as she stood to clear the dishes.

After thirty years of marriage, Alan finally thought he had some insight into his terse wife's moods. He was still occasionally baffled at why she had wanted to marry him in the first place. He was solidly built, and all his features were in the right place, but he wasn't what you might call a handsome man. He'd spent his years managing a small fishery on the harbor that would never make them rich, but that kept a good roof over their heads in the town they had both grown up in.

He had asked her, once or twice, if she ever wanted to leave Bright's Ferry, but she was always adamant.

"I've seen the world, Alan. There's nothing out there that we don't have here, and better, too."

Alan was reassured. They'd been together since high school, with only a brief breakup when she insisted on traveling for a year after college. Then she'd returned to Bright's Ferry and pushed him for a proposal. A month later, they were married.

It wasn't what one might call a passionate marriage, but Alan supposed that a good, solid couple didn't need all those bells and whistles. They'd never managed to have children, but they had each other and that was enough for him, especially as his heart started giving him problems. It was good to have someone to rely on.

Candace hadn't changed in thirty years. She was still solid as a rock, focused on home, him, and keeping the Mayor's Office running smoothly, as she had for Hank Daniels for decades. Alan liked to tease her that she saw more of her "work husband" than she did of him, and that maybe he and Martha Daniels should start a widows club. She took it good-naturedly, but he'd stopped teasing when Hank and Martha were killed. Alan was as horrified as his wife by the loss – they'd been good friends, and since then, Alan had felt Candace retreating into herself, though she looked after Colin as though he were her own.

This recent business with a supposed stalker and Deirdre Small's death was upsetting, and Candace had been ruffled, which was unlike her.

"It's been nice having you home," he ventured, "even if it's for the wrong reasons."

"Colin and Tom are worried that that lunatic will come after me next, which is nonsense."

"They want you safe, and I have to agree with them on that point."

"Well, I'm not going to let some unhinged person prevent me from living my life."

She put the last of the dishes in the dishwasher and reached for her purse.

"Are you sure you don't want to cancel, dear? It might not be safe."

Candace was dismissive as she pulled on her coat.

"The film will only be playing for one more week, so this might be my only chance. Sure you won't join me?"

They exchanged a smile. It was a long-standing joke between them. Candace's year abroad had left her with a great love of foreign film, and one of the few indulgences Alan's wife permitted herself was a night at the local art house. If there wasn't an explosion or a car chase, Alan wasn't interested.

"You go on ahead. I'm going to watch the game."

He pulled himself to his feet and she stopped him in the doorway with a gentle kiss on the cheek.

"What was that for?" he asked, surprised. Candace wasn't prone to spontaneous bursts of affection. They hadn't slept in the same bed in years.

"You're a good husband and a good man. With everything that's been going on, I wanted to make sure you knew that."

Alan squeezed her hand.

"Sure you don't want to take someone with you? I don't like the idea of you in the theater alone."

"There will be tons of people there, I'll be perfectly safe, Alan."

"You said it was a French film? It'll be you and the projectionist," he teased.

"Oh, you," she pouted, with a mock glare.

147

"Call if you're going to be late," he instructed and she nodded.

"I will."

THE ASHER CABIN WAS dark, meaning that Evie was still in town. Colin hopped out of Zeke's truck, flicking on a powerful flashlight as Zeke did the same.

"I don't think we should be here, Mr. Daniels, sir. Deputy Asher was pretty clear – "

"She's not going to find out, Zeke." Colin's voice was firm, which seemed to calm the nervous young deputy, because he nodded. "This is only going to take a couple of minutes."

Colin stepped over to the house, shining the beam up to the porch.

The red spray painted letters were obscene, stretching the length of the porch, over the front windows and door, and Colin felt a wave of nausea and anger.

"Stand over there, Zeke, see if you can light up the whole thing."

The deputy did as he was told, illuminating the harsh statement as Colin took pictures with his camera phone, making sure to get the curves of the letters and the spaces between them. They did look familiar, but he'd need to study them in more detail. This might be a fool's errand. He wasn't even sure that the writing on the wall, so to speak, could offer any real clues about the culprit, but surely there must be some similarities in style – something about the way the "T" was crossed and the lower curve of the "S" triggered a warning bell in Colin's brain. He tried to pinpoint what it was that left him uneasy, but the realization remained annoyingly elusive.

After a dozen pictures, Colin signaled to Zeke.

"Let's get out of here. And make sure that someone comes by tomorrow to clean this up. It's a disgrace."

"Yes, sir."

On the short drive back to the house, Colin examined the photos on his phone.

"Zeke, where are those letters? The hate mail that came into the office."

"Sheriff Arnetto has them down at the station."

Which meant that Colin was not getting his hands on them any time soon. Evie would explode if she thought he was investigating any angle of the case on his own.

Hell, she'll shoot you for leaving the house, Colin.

Frowning, Colin considered his options. He needed to see those letters, but it was doubtful that Tony or Evie would let him just waltz in and take them, no matter how logical his reasoning.

Candace.

Colin smiled. Candace never let a piece of paper enter the office without making a copy or taking a digital print. She was meticulous and thorough, and he could just picture her disgust as she photocopied those letters. But he had no doubt in his mind that copies existed, and that meant that he could get his hands on them with just a little bit of subterfuge.

Behind the wheel, Zeke yawned. Colin felt pity for the poor kid – he'd been everywhere at once, guarding the house, helping with the investigation, preparing for the upcoming Harvest Festival. The kid looked ready to drop. It wouldn't be difficult to sneak past him and the other guards – Colin still had a few tricks up his sleeve. He'd get what he needed from Candace's house, and be back before Evie returned for the night.

No problem.

DREYER MORTON ROLLED OFF of Candace Wilkinson, panting, as she calmly sat up and reached for her dress. He leaned back against the pillows and scooped up his pipe and lighter on the night stand.

"That's a filthy habit, Dreyer," Candace remarked, and he watched in fascination as she swiftly groomed herself, erasing all traces of their tryst as though it had never happened.

"I'm old," he insisted, "Indulge me."

"You're not that old, and if you keep smoking that disgusting thing, you're not going to get much older."

Dreyer puffed away, and Candace rolled her eyes.

"Are you sure you can't stay? Have a drink?"

"Alan will wait up. I've already been away too long, and he worries."

"He's a good man."

"Yes, he is."

Dreyer had been sleeping with Candace for ten years now, since his wife had passed, and she never stayed longer than their mutual passion demanded. It was a convenient arrangement for both of them, and neither one had any desire for anything more – Candace would find a romance both distasteful and unseemly. In many ways, she was a cold woman, but in bed, well, he had no complaints.

"That new deputy is something else. Let's hope she catches the killer before Colin manages to get himself killed."

Candace froze.

"Don't speak like that."

"I know you've got a soft spot for the boy, but whatever happens, he brought it on himself."

"You don't know what you're talking about. You are to leave Colin alone. He has enough trouble on his head. And now that new deputy is sniffing around him, too."

Dreyer shook his head, watching her stiffly pull on her shoes and coat. Candace had always had a weakness for the Daniels men.

"Let the boy have his fun. Besides, illicit affairs? Sexual indulgence? I think we both know something about that."

She blushed, annoyed.

"That's completely different. What you and I have is practically a business arrangement, nothing more."

"There are words for people like that, and they're not pretty, Mrs. Wilkinson."

"If you're going to be disgusting, I'd rather you didn't say anything at all."

Dreyer held up his hands.

"I surrender. Will I see you next week?"

Candace looked him over, haughty, and for a moment he felt like a specimen under a microscope.

"Of course."

"I've had to hand over security tapes to Sheriff Arnetto, but don't worry, there's no hint of our little indiscretions – they're out of the relevant timeframe anyway. But I will be putting additional security on the house, just in case. Not locals. Professionals out of Boston. You can count on their discretion."

Candace started to As she walked out the door, Dreyer wondered if Alan ever suspected that his wife had been fucking another man for years, and then dismissed it. Candace would never permit that to happen. She loved the people in her life like a lioness protecting her cubs. Dreyer could be confident in thinking that no matter what she had to do to accomplish it, Alan would never find out.

CHAPTER FOURTEEN

THE DOOR SHOULD NOT be open, Colin thought, worried as he stepped from his truck and up to the Wilkinson house. Candace's car was gone, which meant that Alan was home alone. His heart had been giving him trouble, and Colin was suddenly concerned that he might have had an attack.

He stepped up to the door and rapped on the frame.

"Alan? It's Colin. I just came by to pick something up. Is everything okay?"

The silence inside the little house on the hill was disturbing, though Colin could hear the muted sound of the ball game on in the den. It was possible that Alan might have fallen asleep in front of the TV. The rest of the lights were out.

But then why was the door open?

Colin edged into the house, a feeling of unease raising the hairs on the back of his neck.

"Alan?" he called again, and headed down the hallway toward the sound of the game.

He found Alan in the den in an armchair, his eyes glued to the screen. But the kindly blue twinkle was gone –

they were glassy and cold. A heart attack would have been less horrific, Colin thought numbly, staring at the blood that stained the front of his shirt, poured down from the gaping wound in his neck.

Alan's throat had been cut.

"Oh, God. Alan."

Feeling sick, Colin braced himself in the doorway.

I need to call somebody, he thought. *I need to find Candace.*

A sudden noise in the hallway had him whirling around, heart pounding.

The killer is still in the house.

Not stopping to consider what a reckless and dangerous move it was, Colin dove back down the hallway – if the killer was making a break for the front door, he could cut them off. The rage filling him was unbearable. Alan had been a good man, a good husband to Candace, and one of his father's best friends. It was clear that this attack was designed to remind Colin that no one in his life was safe.

Colin turned the corner into the foyer and *collided* with someone in the dark. With all of his strength he pulled back and threw a punch, managing to make glancing contact with soft flesh before she twisted away.

The soft, feminine, cry of pain was a surprise, and then an angry growl as the attacker retaliated, and Colin felt a slash of fire along his side.

A knife. Probably the same one she used to kill Alan.

He stumbled back, scrambling to get out of range of the blade, cursing the darkness that prevented him from making out her features, and losing his footing on the foyer carpet, crashing to the ground. On his back, Colin braced himself for the next attack.

It never came.

There were footsteps as the figure swayed forward, clearly in pain, and then regrouped, rushing out the door. Colin pulled himself up and lunged forward, but it was too late.

She was gone.

Outside, the sound of the wind and rustles in the trees mixed with the muffled TV in the den, but the killer had vanished into the darkness.

EVIE ASHER THOUGHT THAT she had never been this angry before in her entire life. Or this scared. She acknowledged that both emotions coursed through her veins, but at the moment, the anger was winning by a mile, as she stepped out of her car. The sight of Colin sitting on the front steps of the Wilkinson home, having his side bandaged by an irate Jocelyn, did nothing to soothe her.

"I'm going to shoot you myself, Colin Daniels!" Evie couldn't keep her voice from shaking as she stomped over to join them.

Behind her, Tony was comforting Candace, who watched in stunned silence as her husband's body was removed from the house on a gurney.

"Get in line," muttered Jocelyn, pressing down the adhesive into Colin's side, ignoring his wince. "You're lucky you don't need stitches."

"It's not like I came over here trying to get myself killed," Colin didn't sound appropriately remorseful, which just pissed Evie off further.

"You're not supposed to be going anywhere at all! Why do I have half this town guarding your ass? All these volunteers, Tony, Zeke – they all have better things to do than to watch over someone who doesn't even have the most basic hint of self-preservation!"

Evie didn't care that they were yelling at each other in front of a dozen people, or that Colin had gotten up to get in her face, scowling down at her. The blood on his jeans pushed a spike of fear through her gut – *she hadn't been there to protect him. The big idiot.*

"You can't just lock me up and expect me to sit back while you catch this killer, Evie. It's my friends and my community she's going after."

"I can do whatever the law allows, Colin Daniels. And that includes putting you under house arrest. Colin Daniels, you're under arrest for obstruction of justice."

Colin looked stunned as Evie pulled a pair of handcuffs from her back pocket, whirled him around, and had him cuffed in the blink of an eye.

"How the hell did I obstruct justice?!?"

"You disrupted a crime scene."

"You wouldn't have even known there was a crime scene here if I hadn't shown up!"

She ignored him pushed him toward her car.

"You have the right to remain silent – "

"Evie, I'm not sure about this – " Even Tony sounded hesitant, but Evie was feeling wrathful, and stood her ground.

"I am taking him home. If he sets one foot outside that house, I'm going to lock him up in the jail cell downtown and invite the local paper to come take pictures. I'm sure that will go over really well with the Town Council."

The ghost of a smile flitted across Tony's face, but he smothered it.

"And we'll cancel the Harvest Festival."

Candace let out a shocked gasp.

"You can't do that! All the work we've put in, all the revenue it brings to this town."

Tony just shook his head.

"My number one priority is keeping the residents of this town safe, along with our guests. If that means canceling the festival, you can be sure that's exactly what I'll do."

He caught Colin's eye.

"But we're not there yet. Colin, go home and cool off."

"You're not really going to let her put me under house arrest. Tony!"

"Sorry, buddy. You're on your own."

THE TEMPERATURE IN THE car was a few degrees below sub-Arctic, despite the fact that Evie hadn't looked at him once since shoving him in the back seat like a common criminal.

She'd actually put him in handcuffs.

Colin couldn't believe it. Not that the idea of Evie and handcuffs in the same room wasn't a combination he hadn't considered a time or two, but the fantasy usually consisted of her chained spread-eagled to his bed while he licked caramel sauce off her tits.

He twisted, infuriated by the restraints, even more angry that she'd chastised him like an errant teenager.

"You can't just arrest me. I haven't done anything wrong."

She ignored him, though her shoulders tensed up.

"Evie, stop the fucking car and look at me!"

Miraculously, she did as he asked, wrenching the car to the side of the road and killing the engine, but leaving the lights on.

She started to speak, and then seared him with one fury-laden look before clambering out of the car, slamming the door shut.

Colin watched her pace along the shoulder, feeling helpless and infuriated. Behind her, he could see nothing but dark woods. They were off the beaten path, completely isolated. Evie was taking a meandering path back to the house to avoid being ambushed along any predictable routes.

Even when she was mad enough to cut off his balls with a blunt butter knife, she was still thinking like a cop, still protecting him from harm.

He knew she was angry, but she was also scared. *For him.*

Something twisted in his heart and Colin was overwhelmed with a frightening desire to just wrap his arms around Evie, reassure her that he was fine, and then make love to her until all thoughts of blood, death, stalkers, and murder were burned away by the fires of passion. The rest of the world would go away, leaving just the two of them.

His reverie was interrupted by the back door being yanked open, and then Evie grabbed a handful of his shirt and half-dragged, half-propelled him out to send him stumbling against the heated hood of the car.

"You nearly died." She poked him in the chest, hard. Her eyes were huge in the dim light, her body close enough that her hip brushed his swelling cock. Adrenaline and fear and anger were having a predictable result on his body.

"But I didn't," he insisted.

"Do you know how I felt when your call came in?"

"Helpless? Frustrated? I'm familiar with the sensations. That's exactly how I feel when you put yourself in danger, Evie."

"Yes, but I'm trained to do exactly that. You're a civilian. I can't believe I have to remind you that I'm the one with the gun!"

"You can't catch this woman on your own."

Her hands came up to his chest. He wasn't sure she was even aware of the move.

"I can't catch her if I'm spending all my time worrying about you."

"Well, you've got me where you want me now, tied up and unable to get in your way, Deputy. What are you going to do with me?"

EVIE STARED AT COLIN in the gloom, uncertain. Part of her wanted to keep raging at him, to do everything to convince him that what he'd done tonight was supremely stupid. Another part of her wanted to plaster every inch of her body against his, to assure herself that his lungs still worked by his breath mingling with hers when they kissed, to feel the pulse of his heartbeat in his chest against her breasts, and the rush of blood under his skin as he filled her with his heavy shaft, throbbing with life and heat. Alive.

You're going to regret this later, remarked the inner cop, but Evie wasn't listening as her hands started on the buttons of his shirt.

Colin didn't speak, but watched her, his breath coming hard, his incredible body passive under her hands. The way he'd made her give up control the last time they were together was masterful, but it was her turn now, and the thought of having him at her mercy, *finally*, was heady.

Evie spread his shirt wide. The headlights cast the sculpted muscles of his torso into sharp relief. She licked the line that separated the impressive ridges, and then abruptly sank her teeth into one tough pectoral.

"Shit."

Colin arched under her, pressing her mouth harder against his chest, his swollen cock harder against her stomach.

Evie let him go, staring at the mark she'd made, shocked at herself even as satisfaction threaded through her – *mine*. Any other woman who saw him now would know that he'd been branded and claimed. *Don't touch.* Evie scowled at the idea of other women seeing his chest.

"Dammit," she muttered.

Colin, panting and tight, still managed a smirk.

"Do you want me to tattoo your name across my ass? That might be a little more permanent."

"Shut up."

Evie pulled his head down for a kiss, hot and wet and seductive, tongues tangling, teeth scraping, breath mingling as she realized with a start that he was becoming her drug of choice – a craving, impossible to kick, addictive temptation personified. She wasn't comfortable with the idea, so she focused on the moment – the heat of his mouth and skin, the rasp of stubble, and the thickness of that luscious cock swelling between them.

She scraped her nails up the length of his erection through the denim, her pussy already wet in anticipation. Colin yanked his mouth away and let his head fall back against the hood of the car with a *thunk*.

"Are you going to fuck me or not?" His voice sounded aggravated. "Because if you're not, at least take out my cock so that I don't come in my pants like a fifteen-year-old with his first dirty magazine."

Evie's breath hitched at the thought – Colin straining against the handcuffs, his jeans pulled low, letting her watch as he let go, his come splattering those rock hard abs and chest, the heat in his eyes an inferno.

His groan pulled her out of her reverie.

"God, you love the idea, don't you? Fine, you can tie me down and watch me come for you every day of the week if you want to. Right now, just touch me."

Drawing out the moment, Evie undid his belt buckle, unsnapped his jeans, and carefully drew the zipper down. Her hands moved to his hips to tug jeans and underwear down over his ass, freeing the hard shaft and the heavy sac beneath.

His cock was always a surprise, the width and length promising all sorts of naughty delights. Feather light, Evie swirled a finger around the head.

"So you are packing a weapon after all. My mistake."

Colin laughed, but it became a moan as her nimble fingers trailed down to cup his balls, gently caressing. He shuddered.

"I hope you're enjoying yourself, Deputy Asher, because arrest or no arrest, the minute I'm free, your hot little body is mine."

He spread his legs as far as the denim trapping them would allow, giving her more space to play.

"Big words from the man in handcuffs."

She straddled his thighs, the residual heat from the engine keeping them warm on the chilly fall night. Not that she needed it – Evie felt like she was going to self-combust any moment now.

"I don't know where to start," she murmured, drinking in the sight of Colin spread out before her like a feast, his cock rampant and straining, the damp tip glistening.

"Put your mouth on me." His voice was tight.

With a tiny grin, Evie leaned forward and kissed the tip of his nose, letting her pussy rub the ridge of his erection. *Yum.* His snarl of frustration became a choked groan as she slithered down to repeat the delicate caress on the head of his cock.

"For fuck's sake, Evie – "

The rest of his exclamation was lost in incoherent babble as she licked a luxurious path from root to tip before opening her mouth wide to take the head of his cock, and then more. She steadied herself with one hand on his abs and found them tight and trembling. Not altering the slow rhythm she had set, Evie looked up to see Colin straining to hold his head up despite his arms being trapped under him, his spine gently arched.

He was watching her. The knowledge had her pussy pulsing. She pulled her hair out of the way and wrapped a hand around the base of his shaft to tilt it, adjusting her angle so that he would have an unobstructed view of her sucking his cock. The taste of him was as she remembered – hot and earthy and exciting, velvet poured over steel. She swirled her tongue around the head and took as much as she could, uncaring that his size made taking all of him impossible.

She thought she was in control until he whispered, low and rough, "Sweet Evie, the way you suck me. Take a little more, baby, and I'll give you everything I have. Is that what you want? Want me to fill your mouth?"

Evie was a little shocked when a whimper escaped her throat, the erotic words pushing her closer to the edge as Colin sneakily took control back from her, rocking his hips up with sexy little thrusts that pushed his throbbing flesh to the back of her throat. She struggled to control her gag reflex, breathing carefully, wanting him to explode for her. *Wanting it all.*

Colin's movements became less controlled, and with her free hand, Evie cuddled and petted his balls, paying special attention to the soft skin behind them. They were drawn up tight. Above, his body was hard, sheened with sweat, the hottest thing she'd ever seen.

"God, Evie – " he bit out, and then he exploded in a rush, filling her mouth as he had promised. Evie took it all, his pleasure pushing her almost to the point of climax herself. When he was done, he collapsed back in a limp sprawl, and she lapped gently at the head of his cock, marveling that it had barely flagged. *Oh, the possibilities.*

"I hope you're not done having your wicked way with me," he murmured, looking up, his eyes brimming with satisfaction.

Evie pressed soft kisses to his abdomen and then slid off to shuck her jeans and panties.

"Not afraid of getting arrested for indecent exposure, Miss Asher?"

"Right now I wouldn't have a problem with it if you decided to fuck me on the main stage at the Harvest Festival."

They both sucked in a breath as her wet core slid against his bare cock.

"Please tell me there's a condom in your wallet," she moaned, relieved when he nodded.

She dug it out and dropped it on his chest, and then tugged the wide neck of her long-sleeved tee shirt down, along with the cups of her bra, tucking them under her breasts to display and frame the mounds and the tight nipples.

Evie braced her hands on the hood and bent over to rub the hard little nubs over Colin's chest, electricity zinging through her at the contact as his cock jerked beneath her, hardening another inch.

"Fucking tease," he groaned.

She was back in charge, and Evie couldn't hold back a grin. She cupped one breast, holding it up to his mouth.

"Suck," she ordered.

Nothing could have pleased her better than the worshipful, "Yes, ma'am" before he went wild for her, sucking and nipping and reveling in her breasts until she was panting, rolling her hips to let her swollen clit ride the ridge of his cock.

"I can feel your hot juices sliding down my dick, baby," he muttered, letting her nipple go with a soft 'pop,' "Put me inside."

Hands practically shaking, Evie sheathed him with the condom and then positioned herself over the throbbing shaft.

"All mine," Evie murmured, the words just slipping out against her will, but she couldn't dwell on it because the broad crown of his cock was parting her folds, luring her down until she was fully impaled. And then she just couldn't think at all, because he was hot and big and letting her fuck him exactly how she wanted to, her pussy filled to bursting with every decadent stroke.

And if that weren't enough to incinerate her control, the look in his eyes as he watched her take him would have done the trick. She rode him until she came, crying out her pleasure, her head falling back. She thought she was done, but he simply gritted out, "Again," his cock still rock hard inside her as he held on and she started moving, fresh shards of pleasure tearing through her system.

"Touch yourself, Evie. Show me what you like. If my hands were free, I'd roll those tasty little nipples and stroke your sweet clit until you shattered for me."

And so she did, touching and teasing her most sensitive flesh while he watched her. When she couldn't take it one more moment, she swooped down to capture his lips as pleasure crashed over them both, his groan against her mouth long and satisfying.

"I think this round is yours," he whispered.

Chapter Fifteen

COLIN STROKED EVIE'S HAIR in the pre-dawn light seeping into his bedroom window, feeling like he was getting away with something as contentment drifted through him. Of course, if she had been awake, she probably would have jerked away. After they arrived at his house last night, they'd been too tired for anything more than a three-minute shower before they tumbled into bed. Colin had been surprised at how tight his muscles were from the stint in handcuffs, and reminded himself not to piss Evie off. He grinned as a shard of remembered pleasure shivered through him.

Well, not more than once or twice a week.

At least her gunshot wounds seemed to be healing nicely, though he was sure the healing process would be faster if she'd stop getting shot at and running herself into the ground. He wished he could say the same about healing her heart. The sexual games were all well and good – *okay, better than good* – but with every day that passed, Colin was becoming increasingly sure that he wanted to give a relationship with her a real shot. Of course, it was hard to tell if they'd have anything to talk about when someone wasn't trying to kill them.

The thought had him stiffening, but then Evie stirred in her sleep, cuddling closer, her arm flung across him to anchor him to her side.

This is what I want.

So they'd started with danger and sexual chemistry. So what? The glimpses of the real Evie he'd seen under the porcupine exterior were enough to make him want more. That was the best he could do, but it was more than many couples started out with.

A couple.

Colin waited for the usual wave of revulsion, but it didn't come.

Well, what do you know? The revelation deserved a reward, for both of them.

As dawn crept into the room, Colin swiped a condom from the night stand before easing Evie to her side, pulling her back against his chest. She grumbled as he lifted her leg over his hip, but he slid his fingers between her thighs to stroke her morning-soft folds until he'd caught her attention, and she was rocking against his fingers, making sleepy little sounds of pleasure.

"Awake?" he murmured, gently scraping his teeth along her shoulder.

"Did you wake me up just to torture me?"

Colin chuckled, but savored her sharp breath as he rolled on the condom and slid inside. Hot and wet and perfect.

"Just saying good morning."

Her fingers came up to thread through his hair, tenderly holding his mouth to the curve of her neck as he rocked them both to an easy, gratifying climax.

"Good morning," she whispered back, breathless, as he shuddered in release.

EVIE CAREFULLY PRODDED HER wounds before deciding that the bandages could come off her shoulder. Her side needed a few more days. She'd have to follow up with Jocelyn. The past week was definitely taking its toll – stress and dodging a killer and mind-blowing sex on the hood of a car were exhausting.

So much for casual and meaningless.

She frowned at herself in the bathroom mirror. They'd just have to deal with it. But she was disturbed by Colin's behavior, and by her own. He wasn't acting like someone determined to have a quick fling that ended in friendship. Instead, he kept pushing her boundaries, shoving her out of her comfort zone and offering an intimacy that both lured and terrified her. For her part, Evie was trying to tamp down on the hopeful little part of her that wondered, as he made love to her so gently in the rosy glow of sunrise, what it would be like to wake up every morning, cherished and loved by some who held her heart in his hand.

Not ready! Evie shivered, pushing the thought away.

Dressed, she wandered downstairs, following her nose to the coffeepot in the kitchen, where Colin was flipping pancakes, his expression far too grim for such a mundane task.

"What's wrong?" Evie asked, pouring herself a cup and sitting down at the table, which was already set.

Colin smoothly slid a stack of pancakes onto a plate, grabbed the maple syrup from the cupboard, and joined her.

"Ever been to Rome? Let's go to Rome."

The non sequitor threw Evie for a moment.

"What's in Rome?"

"It doesn't have to be Rome. Paris. Buenos Aires. There isn't any reason we have to stay in Bright's Ferry."

Comprehension dawned.

"Colin, we can't just run away."

"Why not? I have plenty of money. The killer is upset by the way I live my life, so why not just take my life somewhere else?"

He stabbed his pancakes.

"Look," Evie began gently, "We're going to catch her. I'll admit this is not the easiest thing I've ever dealt with, but life in New York was no picnic. Even before I got shot there were drug dealers and rapists and murderers. I didn't let them run me out of town."

Her mouth twisted ruefully.

"I did that myself, sadly."

"Evie – "

"I don't want to talk about it. Not right now, anyway."

"But someday." His eyes were steady.

She hesitated, and then, "Maybe."

That seemed to satisfy him, and he reached for the syrup.

"Anyway, the point is that you can't just run. What happens to everyone you leave behind? Jocelyn and Grace. Tony, Mary, Candace, Tom. Do you think the killer's just going to leave them alone?"

Colin put his hand over hers, and though her heart quaked, she allowed it, twining her fingers with his.

A FEW HOURS LATER, Evie sat in the corner booth at the diner, waiting for Tony, who was up at the house, comparing the handwriting samples from the stalker's letters to the pictures that Colin had taken of the vandalism at Gram's cabin. Colin was sure he recognized the handwriting, but couldn't place it, so Tony was trying to walk him through it, hoping to jar his memory.

She stirred a cup of coffee and watched people come and go. Occasionally one would smile at her, while another would consider her with suspicion or skepticism, and then turn away.

Dreyer Morton was alone in a booth by the window. He noted her and nodded, and then went back to his newspaper.

So much for being welcomed with open arms. Evie had a feeling that her poking and prodding into the lives of Bright's Ferry residents wasn't winning her any points, but at the same time, the fact that she was protecting Colin Daniels was a mark in her favor. The way she figured it, about half the town approved, while the other half was ready to write her off as Laura Asher's troublemaking daughter.

It takes time, she reminded herself. She was here for the long haul, and would just have to find a way to make it work.

The front bell jangled, and Millicent Grayson walked in, carrying a curly-haired little boy who must have been no more than two. The locals greeted her warmly, and Mary hurried up to pinch the little boy's cheek, dragging a little smile from the usually serious waitress. She ushered them to a booth, and as Evie watched Millicent get her son settled in a booster seat, she wondered if she could really be a killer.

She has a crush on Colin. She has no alibi.

It wasn't enough, and Evie knew it, but two people were dead, and they were running out of time. The killer's attacks were becoming more brutal, more intimate – first a gun, now a knife across poor Alan Wilkinson's throat. At least they knew for certain that the killer was female. Evie and Tony had long suspected it, but Evie was willing to take any little shred of evidence that would bring her closer to catching the stalker as a win.

The door clanged again and Candace stormed in, scanning the diner with steely eyes until she spotted Evie.

"Deputy Asher! I've been looking for you."

She stormed up to the table, and Evie noticed that her gait was a little awkward.

"Shouldn't you be at Town Hall, Candace? We've got better security there, and I'd really prefer it if you didn't venture into public areas without – "

"My husband is dead!" Her ringing proclamation brought the diner's chatter grinding to a halt.

Evie flushed, "I know, and I'm so sorry for your loss."

"I don't need you to be sorry, Deputy Asher! I need you to do your job! You've got Colin under arrest up at that house, like a sitting duck."

"It's for his own protection." Evie was starting to get pissed.

"I can see how well you've protected us, Ms. Asher." Candace was contemptuous.

Dreyer folded his newspaper and stood.

"The Harvest Festival is the biggest event of the year. How many tourists are going to want to come to Bright's Ferry with a killer on the loose?"

"We're following every lead, Mrs. Wilkinson. I can assure you – "

"Assure me of what? That our streets are safe? That no one else is going to get killed? Excuse me if I take your assurances with a grain of salt. Maybe we need to bring in real professionals who know what they're doing. For all we know, you could be asking all the wrong questions."

Evie felt her composure snap all at once.

"Here's a question for you. Where were you last night?"

"Excuse me?" Candace's voice was a choir of disapproval.

"Colin's attacker was a woman, and you were conspicuously absent."

"I was at the French film playing at the Fairview, and how dare you – "

"Actually," and a tall, gangly man with thinning hair pushed up his glasses, spinning around on his stool at the counter, "I was taking tickets last night, and I didn't see you, Candace."

And now the whole room was staring at Candace, and Evie felt a real prickle of intuition as the gears started to realign in her head.

Candace sputtered.

"This is preposterous! I could never kill anyone, much less Alan!"

"She was with me."

The whole room gasped as Dreyer Morton stepped up to take Candace's arm. The moment was almost theatrical. Candace permitted the support for all of thirty seconds, taking in the shocked and curious looks of the people who had known her her whole life, and then she stumbled toward the door.

Evie stood, intent on going after her, but Dreyer blocked her path.

"Leave Candace alone."

"Get out of my way."

"The woman just lost her husband. Show some respect!"

He sneered down at her.

"You've been nothing but a blight on this town since the day you arrived. Not surprising. Do you all remember Laura Asher?"

Evie's heart sank as a dozen heads nodded eagerly.

"A promiscuous girl. A drug addict. Ultimately, a murderer. This woman who is supposed to serve as a role model for our community was raised by a drunk who couldn't remain faithful to his wife, who had no respect for the sanctity of marriage. You would know something about that, too, wouldn't you Ms. Asher?"

"Don't – " Evie began, but the words got stuck as Dreyer thundered on.

"She had an affair with her married police captain, lured him away from his wife. Why do you think she came back up here? They clearly didn't want her in New York. And now I have it on good authority that she's been attempting to seduce Colin Daniels when she should be focused on catching the murderer that threatens our graceful shores."

The murmurs of disapproval were like shards of glass in Evie's heart. She tried to formulate a rational argument, but all she could see were eyes glaring at her, heads shaking in disapproval, and Millicent Grayson, who looked her over with hatred and disgust. She couldn't bear to look at Mary, knowing that the disappointment in her eyes might kill her.

The doorbell clanged, but Evie didn't see Tony until he was gripping her arm, sympathy and anger warring for dominance in his eyes.

"Go home, Evie," he said gently, "I'll take it from here."

"She doesn't even deny it!" crowed Dreyer, until Tony stepped up to face him.

"You'll want to sit down, Dreyer."

"You don't order me around, Sheriff. My taxes support your department, and – "

Tony said nothing, but the look in his eyes must have been enough, because Dreyer trailed off, and with as much dignity as possible, returned to his booth.

Tony nodded to Evie.

"Go. I'll call you later."

Numb, Evie nodded and headed for the door as behind her, a swarm of locals descended on Dreyer's booth, anxious for all the gory details.

THE SLUT COP WAS finally getting her due, and while it wasn't exactly as she had planned it, the shattered look on Evie Asher's face was enough to fill one with satisfaction. Now Colin would see the error of his ways as the town voiced their disapproval. He'd no longer feel the urge to slide between the slut cop's thighs and gorge himself on her toxic flesh. He'd finally be the man she'd dreamed of, the one she'd watched grow up, a better man than his father. Clean and wholesome and pure, just for her.

It was all coming together.

COLIN HUNG UP THE phone for the fifth time and cursed the fact that his number was listed in the local phone book. He felt a little dazed by the onslaught of worried calls from Bright's Ferry residents – the preacher, the mail carrier, his third grade schoolteacher Mrs. Taylor. So many people who had listened to Dreyer spewing the worst of Evie's life out to the public and offering nothing but judgment and condemnation. Suddenly running off to Rome seemed like a fantastic idea.

Rationally, he knew that Evie had support, too. Tony knew her past and didn't seem to care, and Colin was sure that Grace and Jocelyn would stand by her, no matter what. But the timing couldn't have been worse, and now the town would spend less time on the lookout for anything out of the ordinary and more time second-guessing every move Evie had made since she came to town.

Tony had called a little while ago to explain everything, and Colin waited in vain for Evie to show up. After an hour, he realized that she wasn't coming, and that just pissed him off. She wasn't answering her phone.

A couple of antsy phone calls later, Colin was reaching for his keys. It irked him to discover that Evie had chosen to go back to her cabin instead of coming to him, but at least she had had the presence of mind to commandeer Zeke and a volunteer from his security detail to watch her house. He wasn't going to let her weather the storm alone, sitting at home wallowing in self-pity, or worse, packing her things to leave Bright's Ferry behind.

He opened the door…to find Candace on the other side.

"Colin, we must talk."

"This isn't the best time, Candace." He wasn't thrilled with her, but attributed her outburst to grief over Alan's death. Colin couldn't process the idea that she was sleeping with Dreyer Morton – the idea was off-putting, like realizing that your parents still slept together.

He scooted around her and headed for his truck, turning back as the three guards scrambled around him.

"I'm just going over to the Asher cabin. There's already a detail up there, so why don't you go on home, guys? I'll call when I'm heading back this way."

"Uh, Colin, you're kind of under house arrest," one of the guards muttered, scratching his neck.

"And I'm going to sleep with the deputy who arrested me. Anybody have a problem with that?" Colin's temper was frayed, and the blunt words did the trick, because the guards slunk back in a chorus of sheepish denials.

Candace wasn't so accommodating. She hurried up to him, moving stiffly.

"So it's true? You're actually having an affair with that woman?"

Colin wrenched the door to his truck open.

"It's hardly an affair, Candace. We're both single. An affair implies that someone is being cheated on, which is not the case."

"You were with Deirdre Small!"

"What Deirdre and I had was casual. Either one of us could have broken it off at any time. And you're one to lecture me on infidelity, Candace. This is – " He paused, trying to think of a suitable definition.

Candace reddened, but pressed on.

"The woman is a menace, Colin. What would your parents say?"

"I think they'd be glad that I've finally found someone I think I can be happy with."

Candace practically snarled.

"There are better women out there for you, Colin. You don't want to waste time on someone so corrupt."

Colin stared at her, surprised. Candace was a stern and prudish woman – that was no secret. *Maybe not so prudish*, he amended to himself, thinking about her dalliance with Dreyer Morton.

You never really know what's under the surface.

"I'm sorry you feel that way. If you need me for anything, I'll be up at the Asher cabin, comforting my girlfriend. She's had a crappy day."

He left her standing, shocked, in front of the house as he drove away.

Chapter Sixteen

EVIE COULDN'T STOP CRYING. It was as though a dam had burst, and all the stress and pain of the last few months – *Hell, of her entire life* – had gushed out, leaving her a watery, washed out mess. She sat in the living room with a pint of ice cream, wallowing in all the ways she'd screwed up, and wondering if leaving town might not be best for everybody.

Her words from this morning came back to her and she thought of all the lives that would be in danger if the killer wasn't caught – Jocelyn, Grace, Tony, Colin. The thought of Colin had fresh tears welling up.

He's probably trying to explain to his adoring population why he got mixed up with a useless cop with bad judgment and a giant red SLUT painted on her house.

Evie scooped another bite of butter pecan, knowing that her time to drown in self-pity was limited. At some point, Colin was going to show up, and things would just go downhill from there.

Can you break up with someone you weren't technically dating? she wondered, morose.

A glob of ice cream dropped to her shirt and Evie stared at it for a moment before putting the ice cream down and yanking the shirt over her head. She carefully undid the dressing on her side, assessing the stitches.

"Fuck it," she murmured, "I want a bath."

COLIN JERKED THE TRUCK to a halt in front of Evie's house, pleased to see Zeke and one guard standing watch outside the house.

Zeke shook his head as Colin approached.

"Heard some awful things about Deputy Asher. Amazing how folks'll pry into things that are none of their business. She's a fine person."

The tension coiling in Colin's stomach eased a fraction.

"Yes, she is. And she's lucky to have you watching her back, Zeke Biggs."

Zeke reddened, pleased by the compliment.

Colin hurried up to the door, a shiver of revulsion snaking up his spine at the painted slur that marred the front of the cabin. He'd have to take care of that. Not bothering to knock, he stepped inside.

"Evie?"

The half-eaten pint of melting ice cream on the counter made him smile for a moment, but he put it in the freezer and looked around, the sound of running water drawing him upstairs to the master bathroom.

She was a vision, lying partially submerged in the old-fashioned clawfoot tub that was slowly filling with water and bubbles. Colin acknowledged that the vision didn't usually include a swollen nose and eyes and tearstained cheeks, but she was still beautiful to him, and his heart rolled over. Her hair was piled high on her head, and tendrils escaped, sticking to her skin in the steam that rolled through the room.

He cleared his throat, and she cracked open an eyelid, glaring at him.

"Go away."

"I don't care what they think."

"Of course you do."

"Okay, fine, I do, but this isn't the answer. Stand up to them. Show them that all of their stupid preconceptions about you are wrong."

"They're not wrong." Evie swiveled to prop her elbows on the side of the tub, hiding all that glorious flesh from view.

"They are completely wrong," snarled Colin, "Dammit, Evie."

He closed the door, shutting them into a world of honeysuckle-scented steam.

"Forget what they think. Here's what I think. You're brave, you're loyal. You're tough as nails, but you're nice to kids and anyone who doesn't seem to fit in. You are the most frustrating, stubborn, prickly woman I've ever met, and you turn me inside out with just one look."

She was staring at him, her eyes bright with tears.

"Shit, don't cry, because I'm barely holding it together as it is, and I'm either going to smash something or fuck your beautiful brains out."

His fists clenched at his side, but his cock jerked hard as her gaze traveled down his body to focus on it. She licked her lips.

"So you didn't come over here to fuck me?"

"I came over to offer comfort." It sounded weak, even to him, but he meant it.

"And you can't do both?"

Colin struggled for control, but she wasn't making it easy. Sex was a great way to make the world go away for a while, and he could comfort her with his body, but he didn't want her mindless and lost to physical pleasure – she could get that from a good vibrator. He wanted her engaged, involved, giving as well as taking, shaking with pleasure because it was *him*, and nobody else.

"Let's try something new."

"There's something we haven't done yet?"

"Oh baby," he rumbled, "there's a whole list."

He moved closer to the tub, but not close enough for her to reach.

"Drain some of the water," he ordered, "Just leave a couple of inches."

She did as he asked and then resumed her position, leaning forward against the wall of the tub.

"The way this works is that you get something you want, and then I get something that I want. No fighting for world dominance."

"We take turns," she whispered, her voice heated, and he nodded.

"Since you've had a bad day, you get to go first," he insisted, amused by the eagerness in her expression.

"Take off your shirt."

He complied slowly, taking his time with each button, watching as her arousal built with each inch of skin he bared. When there were no more buttons, he shrugged the fabric off his shoulders, letting it fall to the floor, and enjoyed the way her breath hitched as she devoured him with hungry eyes.

"My turn. Kneel up, baby. Show me those pretty tits."

She only hesitated for a second, and then water sloshed as she rose, water and bubbles streaming off her luscious breasts. The crests were tight and swollen already, almost reaching for his mouth.

"They ache," she murmured, cupping them for him.

"I know," he agreed, "I'm going to make them all better. But first, your turn."

He expected her to ask for his fingers on her nipples, or maybe his tongue, but clearly Evie wasn't fooling around.

"I want you in my mouth."

EVIE WATCHED IN DELIGHT as Colin's body jerked hard at her erotic demand. To his credit, he reined it in, taking his time as he opened his jeans, tugging them and the soft boxer briefs just far enough to lift his engorged cock and the heavy sac free, framed by the dark denim.

Two steps had him within reach and Evie didn't hesitate, but leaned forward to nuzzle his sac, enjoying the low groan as her tongue darted out for a leisurely taste. With delicate licks, she worked her way up his dick, humming her approval at his taste, raising warm, wet hands to wrap around the heavy shaft as she fed the wide crown into her mouth. She probed the tiny slit with her tongue, delighted when the move prompted a slight buckle of those powerful legs. Drunk on power despite his insistence that they were taking turns, Evie sucked him deeper.

"Easy, baby."

Colin stroked her cheeks, speared his fingers through her hair, murmured his pleasure as she sucked and savored, a slow, erotic tease. Her pussy seemed to pulse in time as he fucked her mouth with shallow strokes.

"So good. Do you like it? Is sucking me off making you wet?"

She nodded and let him go to pump the shaft through her fingers, lapping up the bead of fluid that gathered at the head. Colin shuddered.

"Come for me," Evie murmured, rubbing the crown against her lips before parting them again to take him deep.

Colin was helpless to do anything but obey, and exploded in a hot rush, hotter as she held his gaze while she swallowed, and then lapped his spasming cock with tender strokes, cooing.

"Your move," she teased, placing a delicate kiss on the head as he shuddered.

He just rolled his eyes as he shed the rest of his clothing, and then climbed in the tub with her.

"What do you want me to do?" she asked.

"Nothing," he replied, "You just get to lie there and let me play."

"But – "

"Shhh. It's my turn, and this is what I want."

He eased her back against the tub and kneeled between her thighs. Her eyes darkened as Colin spread her legs high and wide, propping her calves on either side of the tub so that she was fully open to him. In the bright light, she was rosy and glistening, her most private places laid bare.

Evie clutched the sides of the tub, uneasy with his scrutiny, but he teasingly rubbed her clit with the head of his cock, and she arched at the bolt of sensation.

"What are you going to do?" she gasped.

"That should be obvious, baby. I'm going to give you a bath."

Colin grinned and reached for the soap, lathering his hands up before reaching for her foot. With slow, firm strokes he soaped and massaged, pressing into the arch of her foot and she nearly came from the exquisite pressure. Then his hands moved higher, stroking every inch of her until she had melted into a soapy puddle of lust. He paid special attention to her breasts, of course, and the undersides of her knees, the curve of her waist. Finally, when she was squirming beneath him, *dying* for him, he lowered slick fingers to her pussy, rubbing and stroking and squeezing until she came, crying out.

Colin rinsed her pussy carefully, and then grabbed a condom from his wallet, sliding it on. He came over her.

"Watch me fill you," he said, and she did, gasping as his thick crown slowly parted her folds, her clit peeking out above, tight and slick with water and her own juices.

"I love watching your pussy work to take all of me," he bit out, grinding the thick base against her, buried to the hilt.

He lowered himself to her, and she started to look away, but he caught her chin.

"No, baby. Look at me."

And he started moving, her soapy skin making each stroke a sensuous, slippery glide. Through it, he held her gaze, and she was fascinated by the roiling emotion in his hazel eyes as he filled her body with his own, pushing them higher and higher. When she climaxed again, it was in a rolling, endless wave of delight as he followed and cried out her name.

Spent, Colin reached behind to turn the water back on, and then settled back over Evie, wrapping her legs around him in a snug embrace.

She didn't realize she was frowning until he stroked the little crease between her eyebrows and tenderly kissed her lips.

"Your turn. What is it you want, Evie?"

That was a loaded question. She wasn't ready to answer, but he seemed to realize that, and seemed satisfied with her mouth on his.

For the moment.

NO NO NO NO! He went to her anyway. Reviled and scorned by the town *at last* and Colin, the stubborn, stupid man, had chosen to ignore all the warnings, all the lessons, all the punishment, and immerse himself in filth.

It had finally happened, just as she worried it would. Colin had succumbed, and drastic action had to be taken to bring him back to the light.

How could he not see what was right in front of his face? That Evie Asher was poison. That she was worthless.

Not half the woman that I am.

Hank Daniels had never seen it either, and had spent decades adoring that simpering wife of his while she lurked in the background, never making waves, keeping the town running.

It was her turn to have happiness, to have one of the Daniels men acknowledge her true worth. No matter what she had to do.

COLIN AND EVIE, DRY and clothed, had just stepped out on the porch to consult Zeke about pizza toppings when Evie's cell phone rang. She stared at it for a second in disbelief – coverage out here was spotty at best, and she'd gotten used to endless missed calls and messages.

"Hello?"

"Deputy Asher? This is Zoe with the Shoreline Pharmacy? You called a few days ago to ask about a prescription that was transferred to us by mistake?"

"Yes, I thought we confirmed that."

"We did, but I was just going through the week's records and noticed that there was a second page. I'm so sorry, I should have caught it the first time."

"What are you saying?"

"The prescription order did get sent to us by mistake, but the doctor called to correct the error almost immediately, and the prescription was sent to Bright's Ferry as usual. So the customer would have received a notice about the initial order, and a second one about the correction."

"We didn't question Jocelyn about Candace's prescription," Evie murmured to herself, as a horrific realization dawned.

"Excuse me?" The voice on the phone was polite, but puzzled.

"Thank you, you've been incredibly helpful."

Evie hung up the phone and turned to Colin and Zeke.

"It's Candace. She's the killer"

Colin frowned.

"That's not possible. We've been over this."

"She said she couldn't have killed Deirdre because she had to cross the bay to pick up a prescription. But the pharmacy says that Jocelyn transferred the prescription back here, which leaves Candace without an alibi." Evie paced, working it out.

Colin was shaking his head, "But she was with Dreyer when Alan was killed."

"She was with him last night, but that doesn't mean anything. How long does it take to slit a man's throat when he doesn't see you coming? She could have left Dreyer's, hidden her car, snuck in to kill Alan, and then arrived just in time to play the grieving widow."

Zeke's eyes were wide, and he gulped.

"This morning, she was walking stiffly. Colin, you said you struck the woman you ran into in the dark, right?" Evie questioned Colin, insistent.

Colin was starting to waiver, and doubt crept into his eyes.

"I can't believe it. Candace?"

"You should compare the handwriting," Zeke piped up, and Evie and Colin turned to stare at him, "I mean, she's always writing notes for you and stuff, Mr. Daniels. Right? Even if she tried to hide it, those notes are going to show some similar things."

Evie stepped up to the young man and kissed his cheek. He flushed beet red.

"You're a genius, Zeke. Call Tony and tell him to bring Candace in for questioning. Colin, we need a sample of her handwriting."

Colin was grim, but he nodded.

"Back at the house."

Three minutes later, they were on the road, and Colin looked uneasy as Evie checked the clip of her weapon.

"You don't really think you're going to need that, do you?"

"I'm not taking any chances."

THEY PULLED UP IN front of the house and jumped out.

"Where are all your guards?" asked Evie, pissed.

"I told them I was spending the night with you."

"Great. That's going to help my reputation," Evie muttered.

Colin just grinned.

"If you want, I can spread the word that sex with a fallen woman is *so* much better."

"You're not helping," she grumbled.

Suddenly, the front door wrenched open, and Millicent Grayson was shoved unceremoniously forward onto the porch.

"Colin!" she screamed, and started forward, but a hard yank pulled her back, and Candace stepped out onto the porch, prodding her with the barrel of a gun.

"Candace," Colin breathed, shocked.

"I warned you," she insisted, her voice low and venomous, "I warned you again and again, but you didn't listen. And I sat here, waiting for you to come back from your tryst with that slut cop, and who should show up? Another lust-crazed harlot, dying to pull you even further into the dirt."

"You need help, Candace."

"*Don't* tell me what you think I need," she spat, jabbing Millicent harder. The young woman was crying now, babbling incoherently.

"Let Millicent go," Evie said, "Let's sit down and work this out."

"It's too late for that. And why should I listen to you? Your mother was a whore, too, and I blessed the day your poor Gram put her in the ground."

Colin saw Evie edging for her weapon and was suddenly swamped with a terrifying vision of her, lying in a pool of her own blood in his driveway.

"Take me," he said hastily.

"Colin, no!" Millicent and Evie were in horrified synch.

"Come on, Candace. You and me can go somewhere and talk this out. That's what you really want, right?"

Candace seemed to consider her options. She jerked her head at Evie.

"Throw your gun over there."

"You don't want to do this."

"Now!"

Candace pulled the trigger, putting a new hole in the side of Colin's truck.

Her jaw clenched, she tossed her gun away.

"Now handcuff him and put him in the truck."

Evie did as she was told, but Colin could see every muscle in her body screaming to act. As she cuffed him, hands in front, he whispered, "I'm going to buy you some time."

"I'll find you," she promised, helping him into the passenger's seat.

"I know you will."

Colin could only watch as Evie stepped back, keeping a cautious eye on Candace as she closed the door and stepped back. Holding Millicent as a shield, Candace edged around to the driver's side before flinging her away. Millicent landed in the gravel, hard, crying out as the sharp edges tore her hands and knees. Candace ignored her, her gun trained on Evie.

"You ruined him," she said.

Colin could see the intent in Candace's face.

"No!" he screamed, and kicked the driver's side door open just as she pulled the trigger.

CRACK!

Evie screamed and went down, and Colin watched in shock. His worst fear was coming true, right before his eyes.

Candace climbed in and peeled out, driving one handed, her gun trained on his groin.

"Try anything and I'll permanently disable that cock you use so freely."

Colin looked back over his shoulder and said a silent prayer because, behind him, Evie was picking herself off the ground, clutching her arm, and racing for her gun. Down, but not yet out. The relief was so intense it made him dizzy.

"Where are we going?"

"Somewhere we can be alone."

SON OF A BITCH. Evie ripped part of her shirt to make a tourniquet. The bullet had just grazed her arm, but it still hurt like fuck.

The truck had rounded the bend by the time she had her weapon up.

"Shit!"

Millicent pulled herself to her feet, shaky.

"She was here when I arrived."

"I know. It's okay."

Evie kicked the side of the house in frustration, pulling out her phone.

"You couldn't have done anything," continued Millicent, "She was going to kill him."

"She's going to kill him anyway," said Evie, and dialed.

CHAPTER SEVENTEEN

THE DINER WAS PACKED.

"I don't know about this, Tony," muttered Evie, anxiety seeping into her with each scornful look or gossipy whisper.

"The roads in and out of town are blocked. She's holding him somewhere in this town."

"Yeah, but detective work by committee doesn't seem like the greatest idea in the world." Evie flexed her newly bandaged arm, wincing.

Jocelyn's hands had been shaky as she patched Evie up. It was the first time Evie had ever seen her rattled. She had promised the petite doctor that she would move Heaven and Hell to bring Colin home safe. And she meant it.

Tony clapped his hands.

"Okay, people, listen up! By now you all know the situation – "

A chorus of disapproval and shock as each resident of Bright's Ferry tried to express their horror over the discovery that one of their own was a deranged killer. Tony flapped his hands for quiet, and they settled down.

"We called you here because we don't have very much time. Candace Wilkinson has taken Colin somewhere within the city limits, and we need your help to find them. His life could be in danger. I've already got teams scouring the hills, but you've all known Candace for decades, so what we need from you is some insight. Where would she take him?"

There was a rumbling of quiet anxiety as the locals discussed the problem, and then Dreyer Morton stepped up.

"She likes the movies. Try the theater."

There were nods of approval, and Evie sighed internally. Apparently if you were the richest man in town, your reputation wasn't going to be dented by the fact that you occasionally shacked up with a psychotic killer.

The suggestions started flowing.

"Town Hall."

"The library."

Zeke was busily writing down the half-dozen suggestions, but Evie looked at Tony, despairing as the list grew – there was no way they could cover all of these locations.

"It's not enough," Evie said.

"We're thinking as fast as we can, young lady," said a little old man, frowning at her. "And shame on you," he continued under his breath, "your grandmother would be so upset."

Evie steeled herself and continued.

"There's no way the police can search all of these places. We need volunteers to go *in groups*, to check them out. But if you see anything out of the ordinary, do not, I repeat, *do not* go inside. This is not the woman you knew and respected. This is a woman who will have no trouble killing you, or killing Colin, in the most brutal manner possible."

There were whispers now, and Evie could see the indecision flashing across many faces in the room. And then Jocelyn stood up, bless her.

"Of course I'll help."

Grace joined her, but stiffened as Matt Harris followed suit.

"Me too."

Slowly, the whispers turned to nods, and Evie felt a pang as the town decided to put aside their antagonism to help her find Colin.

Tony offered a few more strict instructions, and the groups filed out, promising to check in every fifteen minutes.

Zeke was quiet, absently tapping his list with a pencil. Evie was coming to interpret his expressions well – the kid had good instincts.

"What's up, Zeke?"

"Well, she's not going to take him to Town Hall or the library or any place like that, is she?"

Evie thought about it.

"She's going to want to take him someplace personal to her, but something out of the way."

"Do you think," Zeke gulped, "Do you think he's still alive?"

Evie quaked inside, but nodded, firm.

"She doesn't really want him dead. She wants him to understand and agree with her. She's only going to kill him if he gives her what she wants and she has no more use for him. Or if he pushes her to the point that she just can't stand it anymore."

For once in your life, Colin, don't push back, she prayed.

Mary was still leaning on the counter, thoughtful.

"I've known Candace my whole life. She always was a cold thing, but I never thought she'd do something like this."

"What was she like as a child?"

"Quiet. Clean. I never saw such a neat child. Her mama was the same. Died when she was a teenager. Word was she fell down the stairs and broke her neck, but we always figured that bastard husband of hers was to blame. Can't tell you the times I saw him pushing her around, and

189

Candace was always covered in bruises. He died in an accident down at the docks while she was in college."

"He was a fisherman?" Evie struggled, trying to put all the pieces together. She wasn't surprised to learn that Candace had had a difficult childhood – that always left scars of some sort, as she was well aware. Of course some people managed to rise above it, to escape into adulthood and get a fresh start. She reasoned that only a very few became homicidal maniacs.

"Not a fisherman. He managed that fishery. Alan took it over after he died, so it wasn't too surprising that she married him. For continuity and all."

Tony raised his eyebrows, saying, "The fishery's empty. Plenty of ways to kill someone there and toss the body without getting caught."

"And it's a place that would remind her of how she grew up," remarked Evie.

"Let's go," said Zeke.

COLIN PRIED HIS SWOLLEN eye open as his uninjured one adjusted to the gloom. The smell of dead fish and saltwater was intense, and he realized that the warehouse was in fact, Alan's small fishery down by the harbor.

Candace had pulled off the side of the road and knocked him out, and then apparently dragged into the back of the truck. She was much stronger than she looked, and he vaguely recalled his body hitting the deck outside the building. Once she'd gotten him inside, the whirr of machinery disturbed him again, but before he could make sense of it, she'd delivered a vicious kick to his head that sent pain searing through his body before blissful blackness overtook him.

Now, he pried his eyes open, and then realized that he was naked from the waist up, and that he couldn't move. She'd exchanged the handcuffs for rope and attached him to the system designed to lift heavy fish nets from the boats for sorting. The hook was on a grid, allowing it to move around the warehouse with freedom, so Colin dangled six inches off the ground in the middle of the room, completely helpless.

"Candace," he rasped, his voice weak. He licked his lips and tried again. "Candace!"

She stepped out of the gloom, neat and calm as always, not a hair out of place, the woman he'd known his whole life.

Well, except for the crazy eyes. Those were new. And the fish hook.

The hook was huge, steel, and sharp, with a worn wooden handle.

"Good, you're awake, Hank. I want to talk to you before this goes any further."

"Colin. It's Colin, not Hank."

Candace shook her head as though to clear the cobwebs, and frowned.

"Yes, of course. Hank is dead. Colin is alive. Hank is dead."

"Please let me go, Candace. Let's discuss this, and then everything can go back to normal."

"Normal? You mean invisible, don't you?"

She scraped the edge of the fish hook along his spine and he flinched at the feel of cold steel against his skin.

From the corner of his eye, Colin caught a flash of movement in the far corner of the room.

Evie.

He had to keep Candace distracted.

"You were never invisible, Candace."

"I kept your calendar, I made sure you ate, I made sure that the leeches in this town didn't suck you dry with their stupid, stupid little problems, Hank. For twenty-five years I was your wife, without any of the benefits."

"I should have paid more attention to you," agreed Colin, "I'm sorry."

"You should have loved me! Instead, you stayed with that clinging woman. Martha was never good enough for you, and I kept waiting for you to realize it."

Vicious, she slashed the hook across Colin's shoulder and he gritted his teeth as he felt the skin split, and warm blood trickled down his back.

"And I watched Colin grow up," she said, nostalgic, "and I thought, someday I'll have another chance."

"But you had Alan."

"Alan?" Candace scoffed, "Alan wasn't a man. He was a pet who kept a roof over my head and didn't seem to care that he couldn't please a woman to save his life."

She traced a finger through the blood on Colin's shoulder.

"Daddy always said that the boys wanted a nice girl. A girl who could cook. A girl who was polite and knew how to keep her mouth shut. A girl who could keep a secret, because people are always trying to pry into things that don't concern them. "

Candace came around to Colin's front, rubbing her arm as though from a remembered hurt.

"But they didn't. They wanted the sluts. The ones that wore short skirts and tight sweaters, that tempted them with their round flesh and filthy lusts."

Suddenly coming out of her daze, she whirled on Colin again, frowning.

"You hit me," she accused Colin, "How could you do that?"

"I didn't know it was you. It was dark."

"And now she's ruined you. Forever."

She stepped behind him again, placing the tip of the hook at his heart, and fear filled Colin. Fear like he'd never felt before.

"Drop the hook, bitch."

EVIE MOVED OUT OF the shadows, her heart pounding, her weapon trained on Candace's head. With Colin in front of her, she didn't have a clear shot.

Dammit.

She'd come in alone, worried that a full-on assault would prove fatal to Colin. They had no idea what Candace was doing to him in that warehouse. Tony had reluctantly agreed, and hurried to set up a perimeter. No matter what, Candace wasn't going anywhere.

"You're not welcome here." Candace frowned, and pressed the hook lightly into Colin's skin. He gasped, and a small trickle of blood flowed down his chest. "Stay back, or I'll kill him. And then you can feel what I've felt. Alone. Rejected."

"You don't want to kill Colin," Evie breathed.

"You don't know what I want!" Candace screamed.

"You want to kill me."

Candace paused, letting the idea filled her brain.

"Yes," she said earnestly, "I really do."

"Because I seduced him."

"Evie, stop it," begged Colin.

Evie edged closer, keeping a careful eye on the sharp hook pressed against Colin's heart.

"I fucked him. Over and over again."

"Disgusting," spat Candace, but her hands were shaking.

"He's an excellent lover. Did he tell you? His cock is always so big and hard, and he can fuck all night if he wants to. Mmm...I'm wet just thinking about it."

"Shut up!" ordered Candace, panting, but Evie just smiled, taking a short step to her left. Candace didn't notice, too furious to care. "You're vile, and you don't deserve Hank's attentions. He was mine, do you understand?"

Evie's eyes widened at the mention of Hank Daniels, but she continued, taking another step to the left.

Just one more.

"Did Dreyer fuck you like that? Did Alan? What did they like to do to you? Because Colin has this fixation with my breasts that I think is a little weird, but you know, guys – "

With a screech, Candace, pushed beyond her limit, raised her hook to strike – and at that moment, Colin *jerked*, forcing his body back, and throwing her off balance.

BANG! BANG! BANG!

Candace flailed like a broken doll before she fell to the ground, her eyes cold and dead.

Evie and Colin just stared at each other from across the room as she lowered her weapon.

The sound of shouts and footsteps roused her.

Here comes the cavalry.

She stepped over to Colin and wrapped her arms around him, pressing her ear to his chest to hear his heartbeat as Tony and Zeke rushed in. Zeke took one look at Candace's dead body and puked into the nearest plastic bin.

Poor kid, still has a few things to learn.

"I think my arms are dead," murmured Colin.

A moment later, Tony had found the controls to the hook and lowered Colin to the ground. He sank to his knees with a groan.

Evie couldn't stop touching him, stroking his skin, and tucking his head under her chin so that his breath tickled her collarbone under her shirt. After a moment, he stirred.

"You're the only person I know that could stop a killer just by acting like a total, raving bitch."

"Well, you use the gifts God gave you."

Colin chuckled and held her tight.

CHAPTER EIGHTEEN

CANDACE'S FUNERAL WAS A tiny affair –
just Evie and Colin and the pastor reading a few words
about peace and redemption before Colin scattered her
ashes at sea. The town was still in shock, and with Alan
dead, Colin had taken it upon himself to give her a proper
send off. Evie had protested, of course, insisting that she
had gotten what she deserved, but Colin reminded her that
it was the right thing to do, to bring some closure to the
situation. Evie had grumbled, but in the end had
acquiesced, even going so far as to suggest setting up a
scholarship fund in Alan's name to help out local youths.

As Evie held Colin's hand, watching the ashes
disappear into the harbor a week after Candace's death,
she realized that he still felt guilty – over the fact that he
couldn't save Candace, over the fact that he didn't see her
or love her, in the same way his own father hadn't seen her
or loved her either. His injuries were already healing to
ugly yellow bruises, but Evie worried that he would always
wonder if he could have saved her if he had realized the
danger earlier.

It would take time.

Meanwhile, Evie was having her own trouble
adjusting to life A.C. – after Candace. She had wondered if

she'd ever be welcome in town again, and admitted that she was going to miss Mary's cherry shakes. As the Harvest Festival kicked in, there was no way to avoid going into town, and Evie was stunned to find that she was suddenly a town hero.

Everywhere she went, people waved hello. Well, except for Dreyer Morton, but that was to be expected.

The kids pestered her for details on how she'd saved Colin's life.

Little Brian Olsen insisted on her walking him home from school whenever their paths crossed.

"Seriously, did I step through a wormhole or something?" Evie asked Tony one afternoon, while they were setting up a sobriety point for the night's festivities. Tony laughed.

"You're the flavor of the week, Asher. They'll get bored soon enough and find someone else to worship."

"They haven't gotten bored of Colin."

"True. You may be shit out of luck."

He toyed with his wedding ring, and Evie almost asked about it, but held her tongue.

She did ask Grace over lunch the next day.

"What's the deal with Tony and that wedding ring? Is he married or not?"

"Oh my God, I keep forgetting you haven't been here forever. You wouldn't know. About five years ago, Tony married Nora Allen. She was a new teacher from a couple of towns over, and he was just over-the-moon crazy about her. Two years later, she went out sailing and a huge storm kicked up. The boat vanished, and Nora and the crew disappeared without a trace. Tony was devastated."

"She drowned?"

Grace shrugged.

"It gets weirder. After she'd been pronounced lost at sea, all these lawyers came out of the woodwork claiming that she was a missing heiress, worth millions, and that she'd been married before. Her ex-husband has apparently been trying to get Tony to turn over all of her assets, claiming they were still married, but in the Will she left behind, she left everything to Tony. So she may have been faithful, she may have been having an affair, she may be dead, she may have been kidnapped, or she may have run away.

"That's awful." Evie was appalled.

"I know," Grace said, taking advantage of Evie's shock to steal her cherry shake. "No matter what happened, she left behind a hell of a mess for Tony, and broke the poor man's heart."

"I wonder if there's any way to find out what really happened?" Evie mused, "Maybe we should – Grace?"

But Grace wasn't paying attention. Instead, she was dreamily stirring the milkshake with a straw and watching Matt Harris lean on the counter to talk to Mary as she rang up his take out order.

Evie grinned but didn't comment until Matt straightened and caught sight of Grace in the corner. The spark that sizzled in the air between them was so hot, Evie was surprised that the sprinklers didn't go off. Then he grabbed the bag of food from the counter and turned to walk out the door, and Grace slumped back into her seat.

"You can't tell me there isn't something between you and that firefighter, Grace Mallow," Evie said, fanning herself.

"It would never work." Grace was adamant.

"How do you know until you try?"

But Grace just shook her head.

Evie wondered if she could coax Colin to take the afternoon off with her. Despite the festival, Tony had put her back on half-duty for a couple more days. He was worse than a mother hen, but Evie decided to let him have his way. Besides, she wanted to rest up for the Harvest

Festival Dance that night. She was so excited about it – her first real dance.

COLIN WAS UP FOR playing hooky, and he and Evie spent a leisurely afternoon repainting the front of Gram's cabin. A pleasant, early dinner of salmon and salad ended with wine in front of the fireplace and Evie riding a deliciously naked Colin on the couch. He leaned back against the cushions, his hands laced behind his head, sweat sheening his body as he let her control the pace, fucking him with slow, sensuous movements of her hips.

"You feel so good inside me," she moaned, her head falling back so that the silk of her hair brushed his thighs.

She traced his biceps, which were tight as he held himself in check.

"You're like a fist, baby."

Colin lifted his hips, pressing in a fraction further as her mouth fell open with a sexy little whimper. The long line of her neck was irresistible, and he leaned forward, lowering his hands to grip her hips.

"Ah –ah," she murmured with a grin, scraping her nails on his abdomen, "no hands."

"Cruel," he retorted, but let her hips go to grip the cushions instead, and cruised his lips along her throat, nipping at her collarbone.

"I'll let you touch in a minute, I promise."

Teasingly, she cupped her breasts and then raised her arms over her head, swaying slightly as she swiveled her hips on the downstroke. She watched the heat in Colin's eyes kick up a notch as he focused on her breasts.

"You can't tease me with those sweet nipples and then not let me taste," he groaned, tortured.

Evie arched slightly, keeping her arms raised.

"Go crazy."

"Already there," he breathed, but he pounced, the wet heat of his mouth on her breasts threatening to unravel her in seconds.

"I'm going to buy some clamps for these. You'll wear them for me, won't you?"

He nipped one tight nipple and she gasped.

"In your dreams."

"And one for this hungry clit," he continued, stealing one naughty little stroke of the swollen nubbin before obediently returning his hands to the cushions.

Evie whimpered as he painted a mental picture, punctuating each image with licks and nibbles, and the steady rhythm of his hips rocking in counterpoint to hers.

"I'll lay you back on the bed and you can spread your legs wide and show off that hot little pussy. Then I'll let you watch me jerk off while you stretch it with a fat dildo. I'll make sure it's the same size as my dick, so you'll have to work to get it in, and by the time you've taken it to the hilt, your little clit will be all swollen. You'll be dripping wet for me, won't you, baby? When I'm satisfied that you're ready for more, I'll flip you over and stuff that pretty little ass with cock and then fuck you until we both pass out."

Colin broke the rules, sliding wicked fingers over her hips to part the cheeks of her ass and rub little circles into her puckered opening. He took over in the thrusting department, too, jerking his hips upward as Evie's brain struggled to catch up to the pleasure coursing through her system.

She was caught on the delightfully dirty image of herself spread wide, clamps on her nipples and clit, taking Colin's monster cock in the ass. Did she want that? Would he even fit? He was going to make her crazy, planting increasingly erotic images in her mind, making her wonder about sex acts she'd never attempted or wanted before.

Evie's laugh was tortured.

"I can't tell if you're serious, or if you just say things like that to get me hot."

"Oh baby, I want to do everything with you. Whatever turns you on. You dream it up and we'll try it. Whipped cream and handcuffs, sex toys, costumes, or nothing at all. As long as you're there, I'm in."

Feeling the delicious tension coiling low in her abdomen, Evie leaned back, taking him with her as she eased toward the rug. He lowered her carefully, not missing a stroke.

"Over me," she murmured, "I want to feel you everywhere."

"Yes, ma'am," he replied, and pinned her to the floor with delicious strength, hooking his arms under her thighs to hold her wide for his thrusts.

"More," she moaned, and he gave her more, pounding into her.

The heat and wonder in his eyes was enough to send her over the edge, and her release triggered his own, her pussy milking every last bit of pleasure as they both unraveled in a contented tangle of limbs on the floor.

His breath ruffled her hair, and he lifted his head enough to catch her lips in a sweet, thorough exploration. His eyes were warm and brimming with satisfaction, and Evie felt her heart turn over. Colin schooled his features.

"So, Miss Asher," Colin said gravely, "I know it hasn't been terribly long, but I think it's fair to tell you that despite our unusual courtship I'm developing some pretty serious feelings for you at an alarming rate. As in, I don't want to date anyone else. I don't want to fuck anyone else. I want you to leave your toothbrush at my place and hold my hand in public and make out with me on the dance floor at the Harvest Festival Dance tonight so that every man in town knows you're spoken for. So basically, I'm asking you to go steady, and I thought now would be a good time to share, since I have you naked and pinned down, and your deliciously demanding little pussy is still pulsing around my cock. You can go ahead and panic now."

Evie's first instinct was to stiffen as delight and horror swept through her, but her body was too languidly satisfied to do anything but arch slightly, which only drove his rapidly recovering cock a little deeper. She tried to process it as he peppered soft kisses over her face, nipping her jawline and sucking the sensitive curve of her neck. It was very distracting.

"What do you think?" he murmured.

Evie took a deep, fortifying breath.

"Okay," she whispered.

"Okay?"

Her eyes suddenly brimmed with tears.

"I'm sorry, I wish I could do better than that. Sometimes you're a complete ass and a total control freak, and sometimes you're *wonderful*, but I'm scared, Colin, and — "

He cut her off with his mouth on hers, giving and taking, hot and wet and perfect. When she pulled away to breathe, his grin was like the sun.

"Okay is a good place to start. I'll even let you be in charge, like, a third of the time."

"Two-thirds of the time," she countered, squeezing her internal muscles around him, pleased when he groaned.

"We can negotiate."

And Evie kissed him.

Epilogue

The young man with the messy brown hair flicked the lighter open and closed as he stepped onto the bus and scanned the seats. He couldn't be more than nineteen or twenty.

"Hey, you can't smoke in here," the driver said, with a face like granite.

"I don't smoke," the young man replied.

Backpack in hand, he headed down the aisle until he found an almost empty row, the seat across taken up by a little old lady knitting a sweater in garish purple. The young man found himself arrested by the color, and the old lady smiled at him, her face wrinkled and friendly.

"Like it? It's for my granddaughter."

"Sure," he said, "My…my sister loves that color. I'm actually on my way to visit her."

He flicked his lighter open and closed again and set his backpack down, taking one last look at the Boston skyline.

"That's nice, dear," the old lady said, not missing a stitch as the bus started to move, "Where does she live?"

"Bright's Ferry," the young man said absently, and the old lady frowned in concentration before her face brightened.

"Oh yes! That's a lovely spot. I believe we're passing through there. A little out of the way, though. I remember one time my husband Gordon and I got lost and wound up driving through Bright's Ferry, this was back when he was still allowed to drive, of course…"

She continued, but the young man missed most of it as the buildings of Boston faded into the distance, to be replaced by trees along the highway – the riotous reds and oranges of fall in New England.

He wondered if Grace would be glad to see him.

He wondered if he could leave his past behind.

He wondered if she had forgiven him yet.

Or if she ever would.

And the bus thundered north along the road, toward Bright's Ferry.

THE END

Want to spend more time in Bright's Ferry?
Follow Grace and Matt's story in SAFE FROM
THE FIRE by Lily Rede.
February, 2013.

ADDITIONAL WORKS AVAILABLE:

Hot for Joe

Build Me Up

My Fair Hex

Passion & Pumpkins

Pour On the Heat

ANTHOLOGIES

Hot & Sweet - Beginnings

Email Lily at LilyCRede@gmail.com

Twitter: @RedeLily

Made in the USA
Las Vegas, NV
02 February 2025

17417601R00125